THE DEVIL IS A PART-TIMER!

2

SATOSHI WAGAHARA

ILLUSTRATED BY 029 (ONIKU)

OF CLPL

YEN ON

NEW YORK

THE DEVIL IS A PART-TIMER!, Volume 12
SATOSHI WAGAHARA, ILLUSTRATION BY 029 (ONIKU)

Translation by Kevin Gifford
Cover art by 029 (oniku)

HATARAKU MAOUSAMA!, Volume 12
© SATOSHI WAGAHARA 2015
First published in Japan in 2015 by KADOKAWA CORPORATION, Tokyo.
English translation rights arranged with KADOKAWA CORPORATION,
Tokyo, through Tuttle-Mori Agency, Inc., Tokyo.

English translation © 2018 by Yen Press, LLC

Yen On
1290 Avenue of the Americas
New York, NY 10104

Visit us at yenpress.com
facebook.com/yenpress
twitter.com/yenpress
yenpress.tumblr.com
instagram.com/yenpress

First Yen On Edition: December 2018

Yen On is an imprint of Yen Press, LLC.
The Yen On name and logo are trademarks of Yen Press, LLC.

The publisher is not responsible for websites (or their
content) that are not owned by the publisher.

Library of Congress Cataloging-in-Publication Data
Names: Wagahara, Satoshi. | 029 (Light novel illustrator)
illustrator. | Gifford, Kevin, translator.
Title: The devil is a part-timer! / Satoshi Wagahara ;
illustration by 029 (oniku) ; translation by Kevin Gifford.
Other titles: Hataraku Maousama! English
Description: First Yen On edition. | New York, NY :
Yen On, 2015–
Identifiers: LCCN 2015028390 |
ISBN 9780316383127 (v. 1 : pbk.) |
ISBN 9780316385015 (v. 2 : pbk.) |
ISBN 9780316385022 (v. 3 : pbk.) |
ISBN 9780316385039 (v. 4 : pbk.) |
ISBN 9780316385046 (v. 5 : pbk.) |
ISBN 9780316385060 (v. 6 : pbk.) |
ISBN 9780316469364 (v. 7 : pbk.) |
ISBN 9780316473910 (v. 8 : pbk.) |
ISBN 9780316474184 (v. 9 : pbk.) |
ISBN 9780316474207 (v. 10 : pbk.) |
ISBN 9780316474238 (v. 11 : pbk.) |
ISBN 9780316474252 (v. 12 : pbk.)
Subjects: CYAC: Fantasy.
Classification: LCC PZ7.1.W34 Ha 2015 | DDC
[Fic]—dc23
LC record available at
http://lccn.loc.gov/2015028390

ISBNs: 978-0-316-47425-2 (paperback)
978-0-316-47426-9 (ebook)

1 3 5 7 9 10 8 6 4 2

LSC-C

Printed in the United States of America

THE DEVIL
HANGS ON
TO HIS DAILY
ROUTINE

There's always something about returning to an old, familiar home that fills a person with a warm sense of relief. No matter how luxuriant the inns one stayed at in the midst of traveling, going back to the cluttered, weather-beaten house always provides an odd peace of mind, intermixed with the loneliness of journey's end.

It did not work that way with Hanzou Urushihara.

"Dude, what the hell is *that*?!"

"It is the demonic force collected by His Demonic Highness and myself. There was no place else to store it."

"Huhh?! Your demonic force?! Are you crazy? You guys have got to be crazy!"

"And this is how you're going to greet me the moment you return home from a long absence?"

"Well, yeah?! I can't be the only one around here who's got a problem with this!"

He had walked through the door to find that the cubbyhole he called home was now taken over by...something else.

Finally released from a long stint in the hospital, Urushihara opened the door to his closet in Room 201 of Villa Rosa Sasazuka only to find that the entire upper shelf—which usually housed his bed and computer—was occupied by a large, mysterious, semi-gelatinous mass wrapped in newspaper and vinyl tape. It almost made his eyes explode.

From his perspective, he had been forced into a hospital room with no real clue what had happened to him, guarded so he couldn't leave on his own terms—and when he finally got out, he was effectively blockaded from his own room. Not only that, but the space was now filled with demonic force, the energy he and his roommates relied on for their very lives.

For Urushihara; for Ashiya, who was not only letting Urushihara's griping go in one ear and out the other but was actually deflecting it back with his willpower; and of course, for Sadao Maou, their master and the main rent payer in the group, the lack of this evil power was the whole reason why life in Japan had been so much trouble for them. Right now, though, the closet was packed with so much demonic force, they guessed it was in line with the Devil King Satan's during his boom years.

Urushihara understood that Maou and Ashiya had no intention, at this point, of using this to conquer Japan by force. The idea, however, that they'd just keep this resource idle in the closet and keep living their current lives made little sense to him.

"Dude, Ashiya, don't you think we could *use* this for something?! Like, there's no value to having money or power if you just let it sit! You gotta leverage it!"

"I see no reason why you are qualified to lecture me on the value of money. Consider it saving for the future."

"Oh, so you're just gonna wait 'til you're old and live off *that* 'til you die?! That's all the ambition you've got, Ashiya?! Don't you think we could at least improve our living situation a little bit?!"

Ashiya gave a wholly unironic, puzzled look at Urushihara's pleading. "Improve our living situation? How do you mean?"

"How do I mean…?" He paused for a moment, so thrown by this meek response that he lost his train of thought. "Well, no, I mean…" He looked around the room, still standing next to the giant block of energy in the closet. "Well, like, our food bill, dude! We can live off demonic energy, can't we?! And if we got this much, we don't need to eat at all any longer!"

He leaped toward the refrigerator and opened the door. It contained all the usual suspects: meat, vegetables, fish, milk, tofu, *natto*, spices, and everything else Urushihara knew his roommate stocked it with.

"Food lies at the very core of our lives," Ashiya replied. "Thanks to His Demonic Highness's hard work, we are able to put three square meals on the table per day. There is no need to wastefully consume our demonic force instead."

"Ugh, I… I wish I had a word in my vocabulary to describe how crazy you're acting!" Urushihara slammed the door. "What about, like, electricity and water and gas and stuff? We don't need any of that, now!"

"Can you run a microwave oven on magic?"

"*You* can! You're a frickin' Great Demon General!"

"All right, so you want us to continually produce bolts of electricity in a way that they can run AC-ready appliances in Japan? On a *far* smaller scale than your typical lightning attack, I should add? It would be a very delicate spell, and rather difficult to sustain, I would imagine."

"Ngh… But…" Urushihara fell silent again, before raising his eyebrows and spreading his arms out. "But look at this room, dude! Now that we got our force back, who says we gotta abide by human laws any longer?! I'm not saying we start wrecking stuff, but we can make humans do whatever we *want* now! So let's get out of this crappy apartment and move someplace where we all have our own rooms, at least! And a bigger kitchen! And, like, bathrooms!"

"Indeed, my liege and I may have thought along similar lines a year ago."

"…Uh, yeah, and that's why I can't believe how *sad* you're acting now, General. I *know* how our thought processes match!"

One year ago, Shirou Ashiya had zero experience with human interaction of any sort. The idea of the Great Demon General Alciel, back when he had no empathy at all for Japan or the human race, considering a move to someplace with fancier appliances and a heated toilet did nothing to cheer Urushihara's flagging outlook on life.

"But we have no pressing reason to leave this building, do we?"

"What?! You're the one who's always bitching about the equipment around here!"

Before he realized it, Urushihara's case had shifted from using demonic force to mind control people around them, to using it to make the plumbing work better.

"Yes, certainly, I would like a large kitchen counter to work with. It is too low to the ground for my height, as well. Having a balcony would make drying clothes quite a bit easier. I feel it is not a noble thing to have undergarments hanging off indoor clotheslines in plain sight of Ms. Sasaki when she visits. But the kitchen issue is not a fatal one, and there are ways we can work around laundry embarrassments."

"But, duuude…"

"And besides, exactly where do you plan to move to? Think about it. We have built a large number of local connections here in Sasazuka, and we have everything we need for our daily lives. And look at who surrounds us—Bell next door, Nord Justina below us. How many shared dwellings can you name where all the residents are so intimately familiar with one another? Plus, given that we are enemies as a rule, there is no reason to be particularly concerned about keeping up appearances, as it were. Meanwhile, the mere idea of trying to hide your presence from our new neighbors, wherever we move to, throws me into a great despair."

"Hey! You owe unemployed bums like me an apology for that!"

"I see no need for that whatsoever," Ashiya sniffed. "Plus, we would need to adjust our electricity, gas, and water plans, not to mention work out a TV license, and we would need to hire movers. Our residential certificates would need to change, as well as our bank and credit card contacts—"

"Daaaaahhh!" Urushihara began gesticulating at Ashiya's long list. "That's what I mean! One shot of demonic force, and it's done, dude!"

"And why do you fail to understand," the unwavering Ashiya insisted, "that there is no hindrance to our lives at this very moment that requires demonic force to handle?"

"Why are *you* working on this notion that we have to keep our *current* lives, man?!"

"What are you saying?" Ashiya languidly responded as he stuck a thumb toward the "spare room" that used to be the apartment's closet. "Do you think that *he* would allow us to work outside the standard structures of Japan, or should I say this world, in the first place?"

As if on cue, Room 201's front door opened, despite being locked.

"Well said, Mr. Ashiya! So glad to see you aware of your situation."

"Daaaaaaaaaaaaaaaghhhhhhhhhhhhh?!"

At the doorway was a woman whose broad-rimmed, crimson-red hat was festooned with feathers from assorted birds of paradise, bright enough to make even the dim light illuminating the outside corridor seem to shine brilliantly. Her enamel stiletto heels were just as bright a shade of crimson, matching her flared skirt and a cardigan that was probably a lot cozier and fluffier a few years ago. For Miki Shiba, landlord of Villa Rosa Sasazuka, it was a bit more informal of an outfit than usual.

"I would not exactly call myself 'aware' of my place in human society, ma'am, but I do try to act as rationally I can."

"A fine thing to pursue! And I'd advise you, Mr. Urushihara, to avoid such flights of fancy in the future."

"Is, um, is wanting to move apartments that, uh, fanciful, ma'am?"

Urushihara edged toward the window, trying to keep as far away from Shiba as possible. It wasn't enough to weaken the thrall she had upon him. The purple tint to his hair visibly lightened before the other two, segueing into a shade of light blue within seconds before settling into a striking silver.

"Dude, dude, dude, my hair's doing that thing again! Stop it!"

"Oh, don't be such a stick in the mud about it, mm-kay? It's totally you. Like, a really bold makeover!"

"Shut up! Why are you goin' around with the landlord like you two are friends?!"

It was, of course, neither Ashiya nor Shiba halfheartedly poking fun at Urushihara's new hair color. It was the large, looming man, almost as tall as Ashiya, standing next to the landlord—his hair the same shade of bluish-tinted silver as Urushihara's. He shrugged at the fallen angel, still preferring to wear his I LOVE LA T-shirt underneath his toga despite the late-fall weather.

"Hey, Mikitty's been a big help. If she's goin' out for a while, I can at least carry her bags for her, hmm?"

"Uh, do you *care* about how the optics of all this looks, dude?!"

The old role of guarding the Sephirot now seemed well in the past for the archangel Gabriel. Now, he was just Shiba's luggage boy, and he seemed to have no qualms with it.

"Oh, and we chatted with Crestia Bell just now, and she said that hunk of demonic force is just fine in the closet. It'll help keep your noise from leakin' into her place, she said."

"All of you are just... *Arrrrgghhhhh!*"

Urushihara cupped his head in his hands, unable to figure out whom to lash out at first. Ashiya, ignoring him, turned to Gabriel.

"I knew our landlord was coming to see Bell, but I heard nothing about you. What would *you* need from her?"

"Mmmm, well, like I just toldja, I'm really just carrying Mikitty's stuff for her." In one of his large, bearlike hands was an alligator-skin handbag, once again a bright shade of crimson. "Though I *did* want to kinda hear more of the story from at least one of you guys. I figured having Mikitty with me would help grease the wheels a little, so I asked her to come along..."

He scratched his head and took a step away from the Room 201 doorway—which, between his height and Shiba's ample girth, was completely blocked. Behind him, in the sliver of space visible next to the landlord, was a smaller woman.

"Not that it worked or anything," Gabriel muttered, the smirk clear in his voice.

"Well, I can see why," Ashiya remarked as he sized up the woman. "And Crestia Bell has no particular duty to listen to you, either."

"Yeah, well, she's a Church cleric so she kinda danced around that, but…mmm, that was pretty much what she said, yeah."

"Look," the woman accompanying Shiba and Gabriel pleaded to Ashiya, "I know I don't exactly deserve a prize for the way I acted… but I mean, there was just nothing else I could do… So please, let me see Satan again. I want him to listen to me."

"You may not. I have orders to chase you out if you come here."

Ashiya's frozen voice sliced neatly through the begging of the archangel Laila.

"My liege is a busy man. Emilia, in particular, has been an additional stress upon his mind, and he has just been through what I would certainly call a scarring experience. Given the new business he is about to tackle, I cannot allow any more burden upon his shoulders."

Ashiya had been polite enough with the woman before. Now, he would give her no quarter.

"And I suppose this may go without saying, but if you decide to embark on anything as foolish as intruding in his workplace, I guarantee you will never be granted an audience with him for as long as you both live. If that is clear, I would appreciate if you made good your departure. No matter what you say, my master's feelings are quite firm on the matter."

"Oh, no…" Grief crossed the woman's face.

"Perhaps," Shiba offered, "it would be best to try again later. Attempting to force the issue may not produce much of a response at this point. I am willing to work as an intermediary, but I can't demand they change their mind, after all."

"Yeah," Gabriel said with a sigh, "guess not. Sorry to waste your time, Mikitty."

"Oh, not at all! It's the duty of any landlord to see how their tenants are faring."

"Hmm? Well, I'm glad to hear that. Hey, can I stay here a bit? I wanted to talk with these two."

"Go right ahead. Come back in time for dinner, all right?"

"Yes, ma'am!"

It was hard for Ashiya to believe how friendly Gabriel acted around Shiba, as he offered the handbag back to her and waved vigorously as she and Laila left. Then he turned back toward Ashiya, grinning.

"You're being a bit unkind, aren'tcha?"

"We are demons. I would imagine that is the normal reaction to an angel."

"I suppose that's so."

The sheer sharpness of Ashiya's voice suggested to Gabriel that it wasn't worth wheedling him about it.

"Welp, I've been *reeeeeal* patient with all this so far. On the order of crazy patient, you feel me? And I'm sure Laila knows there's no point panicking right now. Not that she's not, though, given…the, y'know, all this."

✳

Upon rescuing the captured Emi from Ente Isla, Maou and his expedition team came back to find Urushihara in the hospital and Miki Shiba, landlord of Villa Rosa Sasazuka, unveiling all kinds of truths about their universe.

As she had described it by Urushihara's hospital bed, the worlds of Earth and Ente Isla, while two separate planets, were linked together in the same space. That fact didn't seem to change very much at first, but it was more than enough to give everyone new insights on the people, and the events, transpiring between the two worlds. Traveling across them didn't entail some unknown transdimensional contact—they both existed under the same laws of physics, and even if it wasn't possible at the moment, the right kind of spaceship or whatever might be able to complete the journey without a Gate, sometime in the far future.

The same also applied to the "demon realm" that Maou ruled over. The land where demons roamed didn't exist under the ground or in some ancient myth, but in a real-life planet in real-life space.

So what about "heaven," then? Which world belonged to the angels, who never had a problem getting in the way of Maou and Emi and so on? That was a mystery to the denizens of Ente Isla—a mystery, that is, until a certain someone appeared in a human-, demon-, and angel-populated hospital room. That was Laila: a resident of the heavens, the woman who rescued a young Satan's life, and the "mother" of the assorted girls born under the Sephirah known as Yesod. That and—more than anything else—the mother of Emilia Justina.

She had been doggedly elusive up to now, leaving only the faintest hints of her presence to Maou and his cohorts. But when she finally appeared before them, what she had to reveal wasn't some grand new truth about the world, or some legendary talisman that would solve all their problems, or even the path to paradise. It was instead a vast, yawning gap between mother and daughter, one that seemed all but hopeless to fill in.

It taught Emi that all of the assorted strife and tragedy she had experienced in her life in Japan so far was, ultimately, her mother's fault. But when faced with this, Emi didn't feel any negative emotion—no rage or sadness against the absurdity of it all. Her mind was a blank, and it ordered her to eliminate this presence from her life.

To those around her, it may have just looked like a series of slaps to Laila's face, delivered with a complete lack of expression. But that wasn't Emi acting out her hatred or frustration at all. She just didn't want to believe that she had inherited even a tiny flake of what this thing in front of her possessed. It may have seemed like she was looking at her mother, but to her, she wasn't. Until Maou finally stopped her, even her vision was merely a pale shade of white.

By the time she came to, she saw "someone" sidling up to her father, then Maou stepping in between, as if to hide her father and that someone from her. She stared at the texture of the UniClo long-sleeved T-shirt she had on, before realizing that Emeralda was holding her arms back.

She knew they had stepped up to stop her. She didn't know why.

But even so, she understood that continuing to reject this person wasn't something the rest of them would allow. So she left, taking Alas Ramus from Acieth's hands, not saying another word or even acknowledging Laila's presence as she put Urushihara's hospital room behind her.

✳

"You could've heard her out, at least."

"Yeah, right. You know I'm not willing to put up with that crap... Ugh, thank God, my hair's back to normal."

With Laila and the landlord gone, only Gabriel was around to witness Urushihara run a hand through his unkempt hair to check what color it was.

"Well, like, if the Devil King and Emilia aren't willing to talk, then you're just about all they've got, yeah? You were kinda the only other person there at the time."

"Like I care. Not like I got involved in all that 'cause I wanted to. And it's not like I don't appreciate getting the chance to duck out of that boring-ass world. But, like, it's been so long ago that I'm pretty hazy on a lot of it. Plus, *they're* the ones who booted me out without a second thought. Far as I'm concerned, we're even now."

"If I may ask," Ashiya rumbled as he presented Gabriel with a cup of green tea, "why are you going into our apartment like you own the place?"

"Oh, I'm just wondering why you're so hell-bent on not listening to her. And I just *love* how you're offering me tea while staring daggers into me. You teach those kinda manners in the Devil King's Army?"

"This is not for you. It is for the landlord's assistant. If it wasn't for her apparent protection, I would hardly allow you to enjoy the oxygen in this room, much less our tea."

"Now that's just mean. Though I guess it beats the Devil King kicking my ass the moment I came in. Thank youuuu!"

There was not a great deal of appreciation present in Gabriel's voice as he took a mouthful of the near-boiling tea without hesitation.

"Well," Urushihara noted, "Maou ain't the type to drag a grudge along forever once things get worked out, you know?"

"I should certainly hope not. After all…" He chuckled. "Hell, I haven't been in that much pain since who knows how long."

Gabriel might have tried to laugh it off, but the blow Maou applied to him on the Eastern Island after gaining Acieth's strength was enough to nearly kill him. He had been undergoing intensive treatment at Shiba's house in Japan ever since. Exactly why he had become Shiba's servant in the meantime, nobody could really say—or wanted to know, either.

"Being near the landlord doesn't mess with your body at all, dude?"

"Mmm, not really, no. Mikitty's been taking really good care of me, y'know? I'm tryin' to hold back on my holy-energy consumption, what with my body and the kinda place we're all in, but it's not like I need to sling it around too much around here anyway, right? Not in this country. Most of the appliances and such run at the push of a button."

"Oh, not you, too…" Urushihara sat down on the tatami-mat floor, clearly frustrated.

"But say, uh, Alciel, you said something about the Devil King being stressed out…?"

"…" The question made the muscles on Ashiya's face tense up.

"I'm all but expectin' this'll piss you off if I ask, but did something come up? Probably Laila, huh?"

The revelations from Laila in the hospital room had an enormous impact upon Maou; of that there was little doubt. But it was hard for Gabriel to believe that Sadao Maou—so clearly made of tough stuff, body and soul—would be that fazed by it.

"Well…" Ashiya uncharacteristically mumbled.

"Hmm? That bad?"

"Bppph!"

It was Urushihara who very characteristically cracked up at Gabriel's pressing for an answer.

"Ah-ha-ha-ha-ha-ha! You're probably talking about *that*, huh,

Ashiya? It's not like it hurt him that badly. It happens all the time, dude!"

"Silence, Urushihara! You have no idea of the pain my liege bears!"

"The pain? *Pfft*. Plus, he had it coming."

"Um, what? It happens all the time?"

Gabriel grew confused at these diametrically opposed appraisals.

"Though," Urushihara said with a grin, "I do feel kind of bad for him. He worked so hard, and look what happened in the end, huh? He finally got his license, you know."

"A license?" Gabriel wasn't expecting this. "You mean, like, a driver's license?"

"I think he had to present it to his boss by today, so I'm sure Maou's probably a total wreck at work right now."

"…No dinner for you tonight, Urushihara."

"Oh, come on! I'm tellin' the truth, dude!"

"Hold your tongue! We are able to put food in our mouths thanks to His Demonic Highness's labors. Even if it be the truth, such things must remain a secret!"

"And like I told *you*, we have enough demonic force now that we don't have to worry about that dumb crap!"

"You need to better understand the value of an honest day's work! The concept of labor is one of the core tenets of—"

"Work, labor; call it what you want, you're never gonna make me do it!"

"Oh, now you've done it, Urushihara! Your insolence will not pass today!"

"Um…guys…"

Totally forgetting Gabriel's presence, the two Great Demon Generals argued into the night, the time they wasted on it not only bearing zero fruit, but also actively stomping any seedlings into tiny bits.

It was nearing ten PM at the MgRonald in front of Hatagaya station, with Kisaki doing her rounds with the employees about to take off for the night. This included Chiho, manning the counter at the upstairs café space. Maou was with her, wiping down the tables in one corner.

"Y'know," she whispered to Chiho, ensuring Maou was well behind her, "Marko's been looking pretty gloomy today. You know something I don't?"

"Oh? I, um, I…"

All the girl could do was attempt a dry chuckle at the question.

As the rightful Lord of All Demons, and as the occasional substitute manager at this MgRonald location, you could be sure that an effortless smile was never far away from Maou's lips. But not today. During this shift, those working close to him could detect a dark shadow lurking behind the façade. A smile can only do so much and, considering the special attention she often paid to him, location manager Mayumi Kisaki immediately knew that something was off.

Chiho, who was just about to wrap up an after-school shift, knew the answer to her question. She knew it, but it absolutely wasn't the kind of thing for anyone besides the actual man involved to blurt out.

"Well, um, I don't really know the whole story myself, but…I think Mr. Maou messed up."

"Messed up? What, you mean he failed his scooter license test again?"

"N-n-n-no, no, not that, he's got that!"

There was no way the rather blunt question made it to Maou's ears, but it still made Chiho fly into a panic.

"Well, great. We're just about to kick off deliveries, so if the main force behind that keeps failing the exam, it's gonna hurt morale around here sooner or later."

"Ooh, yeah, totally…!"

It wasn't his fault, technically, but Maou had failed his driver's exam twice—the first time because he screwed up the written portion, the second time out of necessity. Both were understandable enough, but given the experiences before, during, and after this cavalcade, Maou had started to see the two-wheeled, motorized scooter license examination as his personal nemesis.

Still, his will remained strong. He overcame the chaos he encountered in Ente Isla, he recovered his old life in Japan, he dealt with his sworn enemy Emi joining MgRonald, and he even tracked down the archangel Laila, the root of all their troubles. Now, it was time for the next chapter in his life—or it should have been. At the very end, mere feet from the finish line, that tyrannical driver's exam had one final, underhanded blade for him to dodge.

"Hmm. Well, I'll try to pep 'im up a bit. Because he's not setting a good example like that, and if something's bothering him, we need to give 'im some support. He's only human."

"Oh, um, Ms. Kisaki...oh."

She left before Chiho could finish, and whether Maou was human or not, this ideal boss—constantly concerned about the mental state of her employees—was about to ask him a question about which she had no idea the sheer cruelty.

"Hey, Marko, how's it going today? It looks like you're just kinda going through the motions this shift, but is there something on your mind?"

"Ah, n-no... Nothing like that..."

"Oh, yeah? Well, you know, you aren't Superman or anything, so if something's up, it's not healthy to bottle it up all night."

"Y-yeah, definitely..."

Listening from afar, Chiho breathed a sigh of relief that Kisaki didn't press any further. Maybe it would work out after all.

"Oh, right, can you let me look at your license for a sec later? I need to make a copy for your records if you're on the delivery crew."

"Ah."

He instantly froze, his grim expression stuck on his face.

Kisaki wasn't the type of manager to needlessly snoop on her staff's private lives, but business was business. As a supervisor, if someone was ferrying fast food around western Tokyo without a license, it would be her neck on the line. But that license was currently the bane of Maou's existence.

"Do I...have to, ma'am?"

"Um, yeah? What do you mean, do you have to? The place is empty anyway, so why don't we go down and get that taken care of? Chi'll take care of anyone who shows up."

"S-sure thing................. *Haah*."

With the look of a prisoner who'd just received the death penalty, he followed Kisaki down the stairs. Chiho could do nothing but meekly look on.

"Maou…"

She could do nothing because she knew what was causing his distress. In fact, she had a fairly similar issue herself—not that she'd told anyone yet. The thing was, even though their problems were similar, the paths toward solving them were like night and day between the two. There were no easy words of encouragement she could find to assuage him.

"Dang. Marko's off his game, huh?"

The muttered observation came from Takafumi Kawata, a first-floor crewmember who watched Maou and his manager shuffle to the back office like a funeral procession. Emi, working the night shift with him, ignored their passage.

"I don't think so," she said, not lifting her head. It was just before ten—the end of her shift, just like Chiho—and she was too busy cleaning up to give it any further attention.

"Nah? 'Cause he's kinda been shambling around the space all day."

"Oh, he just got an upset stomach from some food he picked up off the sidewalk."

"Off the sidewalk?" Kawata snickered. "Y'know, I couldn't help but notice from the start, but you kinda have it in for Marko, don't you, Yusa?"

"I never *didn't*," Emi sharply replied. Kawata snickered again—and that was the end of it, just as Chiho went downstairs. The clock had just ticked its way past ten, and Emi took the opportunity to lean over the counter toward the depressed high schooler.

"So what's up?" she asked, trying her best to be gentle.

"It…" Chiho began, voice just as depressed as her look. "It's the license."

"The license?"

"The photo on the license."

"What do you mean?"

"Ohhhh," Kawata said, banging a fist against his hand. As a scooter license holder, he seemed to know what this meant. "Was something weird with his face in it?"

"Yeahhh…"

"Huhhh?"

Chiho nodded at the question. Emi could hardly believe it.

"I guess," Chiho continued, "he doesn't really like his license photo."

"Is *that* what he's so depressed about?"

"I don't know. I guess? He had the guys at the licensing center take it. You have a bike license, right, Kawatchi? Is that just how license photos work out, always?"

"Yeah. They kind of bang them out one after the other at the center, so…"

"'Cause the way Maou put it, it was like they were aiming for that exact moment to take the shot."

"Well, that's just how it is, kinda. All my college buds with licenses are pretty embarrassed about theirs, too."

Driver's licenses, as everyone knows, can also serve as personal ID cards, and as a result, the photos on them must follow strict guidelines. No hidden eyebrows; no hairstyles, clothing, or backgrounds that conceal your face or appearance; nothing but a completely blank expression allowed—basically, nothing that would prevent a third party from identifying the guy or gal in the picture. You're free to bring in your own license photo if it follows the regulations, but most license-seekers just have their picture taken at the nearby licensing center or police station.

Given the crowds that gather in Japan's DMVs, the general rule is that if the picture they take follows the rules do-overs aren't allowed. It was therefore often the case that the photo on the license you're handed is absolutely nothing like you anticipated.

"On my student ID, too," Chiho bashfully admitted, "my bangs were all messed up, and all my classmates showed me theirs just to cheer me up, I remember…but for him, I guess it's the nose."

""The nose?""

"Yeah, he said it was, like, the moment he had the nostrils flared wide open…"

The confession clearly left Chiho embarrassed, and given that Chiho made no secret of her infatuation with Maou, it really must have been that off-kilter of a shot. The guy at the DMV apparently liked it well enough, though, so to a stranger, the photo had to be within the realm of human decency.

It was thus unfortunate that Maou chose that timing to walk across the front counter, fresh from (likely) showing the results of that picture to Kisaki. He didn't fail to notice the sly grins on all three employees' faces as he did.

"Hey, show it to me, too."

"Uh?"

"You had a funny license photo, right? Show it."

Maou turned to Chiho, face stricken with world-ending heartbreak.

"Oh, way to stab me in the back, Chi!"

"Ah, I, um, that, I'm sorry!!"

The girl brought a hand to her visor, eyes darting to and fro, before she whirled around and made a dash for the break room.

"It's not her fault," Emi offered. "We forced the truth out of her. I don't have a license, so I'm just curious. How's it look?"

"You'll never know! Aren't you off duty? Get out of here!"

"Geez, it wouldn't kill you to show me."

"No, but it'd kill my self-respect, my life span, *and* my mental state! Go home! Get out of my sight! Or *you* go get a license and have them screw up your pic, too!"

"Boy, oh, boy…"

"Okay, quit the chatter, people! It's still opening hours!"

The stern warning rose up from Kisaki, following behind Maou.

Kawata resented this, given that "boy, oh, boy" was his only contribution to the ruckus. "*And* he never showed it," he muttered. "What a rip-off."

It was twelve thirty in the morning by the time Maou wrapped up closing duties and locked the automatic doors out front. Normally, he'd take the occasion to walk up to his trusty steed—the townie he still insisted on calling the Dullahan II—and stretch out in front of it, grateful for another day's work. Today, though, didn't give him much sense of achievement.

"Goddammit, Emi..."

She'd trampled all over that stupid license photo. It almost brought him to tears.

"You really hate it that much?" asked Kawata, who got off work with Maou and was already aboard his own motorbike.

"Ms. Kisaki laughed at it a little, too."

"Ooh, rough. If it's *that* bad," he said as he put his helmet on, "I kinda wish I'd gotten to see it, too."

"No, man! Ugh, I swear, things have been nothing but trouble for me ever since Emi showed up."

"Aw, why let it bother you? She's been in this huge funk, too, lately. It helped break the ice a little around the place."

"Huh?" Maou blinked. "Who's been in a funk?"

"Well, Yusa, I mean."

"How so?"

"Oh, I dunno, just kinda felt that way to me." Kawata looked up while adjusting his helmet strap, reaching into his memory. "Like, pretty much since right after she got hired? There was this one day when she was super down in the dumps the whole shift. Didn't you notice? Ms. Kisaki was off, so you had to be there."

"Oh."

"This one day" rang a bell in Maou's mind. He didn't recall exactly how she'd acted, but he knew full well what had gotten her down that far.

"I think it was about three days later when I had a shift with her again, but she was back to my first impression of her by then. Like, kinda nervous about something, or…"

"You sure pay a lot of attention to her, Kawatchi."

"Hey, not like *that*," he protested, waving an arm in self-defense. "Yusa's kind of the center of attention right now, you know? Ms. Kisaki's been expecting a lot out of her, and you and Chi knew her from before, too, right? So I can't help but check her out."

"I'd advise against it. She's a pain in the ass."

"I told you, it's not like that!"

Even in the dimly lit bike-parking area, the panic in Kawata's voice was obvious.

"But anyway, Marko, she's your trainee and stuff; why don't you look after stuff like that a little more? She might put on a strong face, but maybe she's a lot more fragile'n that inside."

"……" Maou paused, taken aback. "You really *have* been paying attention."

Kawata and Emi had spent no more than a few days together since MgRonald hired her, but in that short span, he had nurtured a scarily accurate picture of Emi's psyche.

"Hey, stop picking on me!"

"No, I mean, it's impressive. Maybe you should try becoming a therapist or something, Kawatchi."

It was a fairly serious suggestion, but Kawata shook his head as he started the engine. "Oh, no way. I barely take responsibility for my own life; I don't want to be on the hook for someone else's. Never have, never will."

"Yeah, I guess…"

"And yeah, people go up to me with their problems a lot, but, you know, they're my friends and stuff, so I just say whatever comes to mind. There's no guarantee I'm right or whatever. So don't tell her I said that, okay?"

"Sure, sure. I'll keep it in mind, though."

"Thanks. See you later."

Kawata gave Maou a suspicious look for a moment—but just for a moment, before he turned on his lights and roared off. Maou watched his taillight until it disappeared, then scowled.

"On the hook for someone else's life, huh?"

Something about the offhand statement stuck in his mind, as he took the lock off the Dullahan II and muttered to himself.

"Yeah, he's sure got that right."

✳

"P-pweefe… Pweefe, liffen to me…"

Back on that "one day," Laila was lying on the floor, swollen cheeks jiggling as she mumbled in self-defense.

"There's nothing you can say that I'll listen to," Emi coldly replied, staring astonished at her slightly reddened palms. "Get back here. I'll take your head off."

"Waaait! Calm dowwwn!"

"Emi, dude, chill! That'd be even worse for you than killing me!"

Despite Emeralda holding her arms back and Maou stepping in front of her, there was nothing that could stop Emi now.

"Move."

Emeralda had walked the line between life and death with her—and Maou wagered his neck against hers several times—but neither had seen Emi exhibit such cold eyes before.

"*Move.* I'm angry."

"I—I knowwww that, but…"

Her voice sounded like it would freeze the air itself. This wasn't a case of Emi being so racked with anger at Laila that she'd forgotten herself. No, she was seriously trying to hurt her.

"Eme… Devil King…and you, Father…" Emi sized up Emeralda, then Laila and Nord, both located behind Maou. "I've been used and abused by this woman for years, with no idea what was happening to me. I've been in mortal danger, and I've lost things that were so important to me. Not once or twice, but…lots of times. And you guys think I should just let bygones be bygones and forgive her for everything she's done?"

"Well, buuut…"

"She's treated *you* like a pile of crap, too, Eme, hasn't she? Didn't she mooch off you for who knows how long?"

"Umm, all right, yes, that diiid happen, but…"

Emeralda had mentioned, on her first visit to Japan, that Laila was shacking up in a room at the Holy Magic Administrative Institute in Ente Isla. She phrased it like a half-joking complaint at the time. Now, it repulsed Emi.

"But stillll…there's no need to go to extreeemes like these…"

"What do you mean, 'like these'? You aren't defending her because she's my mother, are you?"

"Not juuust that, no, but…we can't let things stay like thiiis…"

"Yeah, I'm sure I'd kill her."

"Emiliaaa," Emeralda groaned. But there was no response or method she could find to stop her.

"Emi!" Maou had no insight into her mind, either, but he felt the need to say *something*, before she started swinging her Alas Ramus–fused sword around. "I know how you feel, but get ahold of yourself! You wanna have your say, and I get that, but does it have to be right now?!"

"I don't need *you* telling me you know how I feel. You know as much as I do how elusive this woman's been. If we let her go now, who's to say when or if I'll ever see her again? It could be centuries, or millennia. And if that's how long it takes, are *you* willing to kill her for me?"

"Whoa, Emi…"

"……"

The two glared at each other in silence. The sight of the Devil King protecting an angel and a human being, and the Hero baring her fangs against them, made everyone in the room swallow nervously.

"…You know I'm joking about that."

It was Emi who looked away first.

"I'm here to defeat you. No way I would ask you to do *that* for me."

"Um…well, look, if you promise to just chill out for the time being…"

"Emiliaaa…"

They had given her far too much space to work with.

A flash of wind passed between Maou and Emeralda. It was all they could do to catch sight of her long hair as it whizzed by. The newly created dent on the linoleum floor where she once stood told the whole story behind her near-invisible speed. The fist raised into the air was laced with a concentration of holy energy that only Emi could conjure, on this or any planet. Maou could only keep up with it in his thoughts.

She was serious.

"Yeah well, take a time-out for a sec."

But the flash of surging light that neither the Devil King nor a Church sorceress could contain was whisked away by a twirl of dark wind.

"You…certainly aren't normal, are you?"

"You're talkin' as if you are."

She could make the holy sword go away, they knew, but Amane Ohguro had just stopped Emi's fist—a fist with enough force to turn a "normal" person's skeleton into dust. A beat later, the unaware Maou and Emeralda turned toward them and gasped.

"E-Emilia…"

"Emi… Emi, you don't have to…"

"And maybe you let your guard down a little, too, huh?" Amane told the other two. "If Yusa was any more serious about this than she is, *he* might've been a thing of the past just now."

"………!"

Behind Amane was Nord, quivering as he tried to shield Laila. Emi was watching him. She knew he'd have his eyes on her the whole time, and she knew he wouldn't just give up Laila for her. Thus, she knew now that even if she could escape Emeralda and Maou's grasp, there was nothing else she could do to Laila.

She was willing to commit all sorts of atrocities on the woman— but not on her father. To her, that strike was just a test.

"I'm going home."

Emi stepped away from Amane, walking past Maou and Emeralda in a daze.

"E-Emi…"

"Mommy…"

After all but wrestling Alas Ramus from Acieth's hands, she left Urushihara's hospital room. Nobody dared to speak until she closed the door. Nobody except one.

"Um, I'm not really sure what's going on…"

It was Chiho.

"But this isn't the first time we've met, is it, Laila?"

"A-are you…?"

Chiho knelt before Laila, still frozen behind Nord's back.

"I don't what happened between you guys…but you were using my body like you did last time…weren't you?"

Everyone else was still getting over the shock of what had just happened. Chiho, meanwhile, was the same as always. She had a smile on her face, but behind that was an inscrutable kind of monumental strength.

"Um, Chi?"

"I'm fine, Maou. Let me talk for a bit." She looked the angel in the eye. "While she was here in this room, what was Yusa…or Emilia…the angriest about?"

"Uh…"

Laila looked at Chiho in silence—a millennia-old angel at a loss for words against a seventeen-year-old human girl.

"When I was admitted into this hospital, you gave me some of your strength, didn't you? And up to now, I really appreciated that. I was really glad I could help Maou and Yusa for a change."

"Th-that…"

It was back when Raguel, the Angel of Judgment, paid a visit to Japan. He had launched a sonar-driven strike of holy magic that rode on TV broadcast signals, hoping to track down Laila after she had absconded from heaven. The results put Chiho into a coma—until *someone* infused her with enough force to defeat both Raguel and Gabriel, the archangel pulling the strings behind him. Chiho had been able to hear this "someone" talking to her. It had definitely been an angel. An angel that turned out to be Laila.

"But maybe I shouldn't have been."

"Huh?"

"You lent me your force because you didn't want to go out there yourself, didn't you?"

This startled Laila. She looked up, then turned not to Chiho, but behind her—to the door. It had shut itself tightly, like it was designed to do.

"I know you're pretty powerful, Laila. At least more than a 'normal' person...like Nord."

"Ah..."

"I know Emilia listens to reason, too, but I can tell that she's got some complex emotions about her mother she's dealing with. I don't know why you never really showed yourself before now...but, you know, you have to at least be there. You can't *not* be."

Laila had no words for this harsh judgment. She knew what "now" meant—that exact moment when Amane blocked Emi's fist from landing. She had to "be there" to take it—to take that blow, so intimately laced with Emi's feelings. Instead, under the collective protection of Nord, Amane, Emeralda, and Maou, all she did was yell at Emi to listen to her—layers away from where they could actually see each other.

It symbolized exactly what made Emi so resentful of her. The way she kept meddling in her life from some unseen hideout, mixing things up and making her life a mess. Everyone in the room knew that Laila was motivated by some greater goal. But if it meant getting someone else in this group involved, then she had to stand up for them, and herself, when the time called for it.

Laila had lost one of her biggest chances—the chance to tell her daughter, Emilia Justina, the strongest human being in the world and probably the universe, what she was striving for.

"You know, I keep telling Amane that I wanna get outta here, but dudes, I really wish you'd all stop fighting by my bed...*oof.*"

Urushihara, completely failing to read the room as always, was stopped cold by a sidelong glance from Shiba.

"Um, I—I..."

Laila tried to put a sentence together, finally realizing the weight of what just happened. Chiho just shook her head at her, sterner than ever. "Don't tell it to me," she said. "I can't do anything for you, and I can't tell Emilia for you, either. I'm just a regular person. I'm Emilia's friend. I can't do something my friend doesn't want me to do."

Without waiting for Laila's response, Chiho stood up and took Emeralda's hand.

"Umm...?"

"Let's go, Emeralda. Someone's got to go after her, and I think you're probably the best girl for the job."

"Y-you think? I thiiiink Bell or the Devil Kiiing would be betterrrr—"

"Hey, why *me*?"

Being called out by name seemed to affect Maou a lot more than Suzuno. But Chiho shook her head at both ideas.

"Maou wouldn't work at all. Yusa isn't about to go sit in a corner and bawl her eyes out—not after this. She's *really* angry right now, and having Maou stroll in front of her would just be tossing gasoline on the fire. He could swear up and down that he's given up on conquering the world, and she'd *still* slash him up. It's gotta be someone she won't lash out at, and that's either me, you, or Suzuno."

It was a pretty heavy-handed analysis, but it somehow made sense to everyone in the room.

"Can you do it, Emeralda?" Suzuno asked.

"Bellll?"

"I will take care of things in here, Chiho. Take Emeralda with you and find Emilia as soon as possible. She needs someone she can vent at without consequence, and I think Emeralda is perfect for the task."

Taking Chiho and Emeralda out of the room would leave only Nord and Suzuno, in terms of human representation. Nord could never be an impartial player—Laila meant too much to him. In other words, ignoring Shiba and Amane, no one besides Suzuno would both be on Maou's "side" and fully understand the situation from start to finish. Along those lines, Suzuno's balance of intelligence and power made her the perfect woman to take that role.

"All right! We'd better get going, Emeralda. Get well soon, Urushihara!"

Grabbing Emeralda by the hand, Chiho sprinted out the door. The rest of the group stared at the doorway, then at Laila. She looked like she had been through the wringer—staring into space, hands on the floor, breathing ragged.

The storm of events had dizzied Maou as well. Being reunited after X number of centuries wasn't exactly an unhappy feeling for him—not at first—but after all these unexpected developments, any goodwill he felt was now flung far into outer space.

It was Shiba who then added a final blow.

"I suppose Laila first came here…oh, seventeen years ago, was it?"

"Seventeen?!" came the chorus back. They had guessed from Nord's testimony that she was here pretty well before Maou or Emi, but never *that* long before.

"Please wait a moment, Ms. Shiba. By seventeen years, do you mean…?" Suzuno took a moment to dart her gaze between Nord and the landlord several times. "…Right after Emilia was born?"

Laila gave a shallow nod. "Because…because I felt they were going to find him…and Emilia…"

She had left Nord's farm soon after giving birth—and when she did, Nord saw a streak of light in the sky, seemingly chasing after her. It was simple enough to shake off these heavenly pursuers before—but not this time. She had to keep Nord and Emilia, and the two Yesod fragments she gave them, incognito. And to do that, she needed to make herself as attractive a target as possible.

"But…once I let them get that close, I just couldn't shake them off at all."

Laila herself may have been an archangel, but she lacked the overwhelming strength enjoyed by Gabriel and the other guardians. In terms of direct comparison, she'd be a better match for angels like Sariel or Raguel.

"So she took off in that one final, mad dash for freedom," Shiba said, "and she wound up on Earth, right here. Well, not *here* here—she first showed up in a suburb of Cairo. Ah, it was such a lovely, starlit night."

"Cairo? Like, Egypt? Why there...?"

"Oh, the Yesod bits in Laila's possession were attracted to us, is about all I can say. My relatives just happened to be staying in Cairo at the time, and Amane was more of an *obedient* child back then, so she showed up at family gatherings quite a bit more often."

"You don't have to put it like that, Aunt Mikitty."

"So you knew Laila for that long?" Maou asked his landlord, who was just as calm and composed as the moment they'd all entered the room.

"And if they were pursuing her, why did they stop?" Ashiya continued.

Before Shiba could answer them, Amane spoke up. "They didn't. We just scared 'em off a little."

"'We' meaning you and Ms. Shiba here?"

"Well, I wouldn't say that's wrong, exactly," Amane replied to Suzuno, shaking her head, "but more like all our relatives did."

"...Wait. Meaning...?"

"Right, everyone in the family of Earth's Sephirah. There were some second- and third-generation people like myself, but it was the whole original gang, too, and they happened to be vacationing in Cairo. I was at my uncle George's place, meanwhile, to go spend the summer."

Amane's eyes turned to Acieth, who was now clearly bored with the proceedings and about to touch some clinical machine by Urushihara's bedside that was clearly not meant to be touched.

"Uncle George is Chesed, by the way. The blue one."

"Chesed? Chesed, he is in Japan?!"

"Whoa! Dude, she pushed something!"

Acieth's vivid response to the mention of Chesed, the fourth Sephirah, made her inadvertently flip a switch on a nearby panel that was obviously not meant for amateur control. Urushihara wasn't a fan.

"No, his name's George, remember? He's a British national on this world, living in Cairo—and he's not gonna be the same Chesed that you're familiar with, Acieth, okay? So anyway, Uncle George invited everyone over to Cairo to hang out. It was me, Aunt Mikitty, the rest of the Ohguro gang... Um, were the Goldmans there, too?"

"No," Shiba replied, "the Hawaii Goldmans had some urgent business that kept them at home, remember? So they just sent their youngest boy, Timmy, over, I believe."

"Oooooh, Tim. He was such a brat. I remember Uncle George buying a toy boat for me, and then Tim broke it, like, immediately."

"Well, he may have been a brat back then, but now he's running the Goldman family's marine shipping business. At least *he's* a responsible young man nowadays, unlike someone in the room I could name. And I thought he was going to give you a new boat to make up for that. A real one, yes?"

"Hey, I run the family beach bar, remember! That's no mean feat! And yeah, he said he would, but he mailed me pics of this, like, huge passenger liner that I'd never be able to find dock space for in Kimigahama, so I turned it down."

Maou let Shiba and Amane catch up on family affairs for a few moments, too dumbfounded to get a word in edgewise. Then a couple of their geographical references piqued his interest.

"Egypt...and Hawaii?"

"Oh, wait, I remember! Harianak from Indonesia was there, too! Me and him tricked Tim into getting on a camel and left 'im to roam the desert for half a day. Boy, was he pissed at me! Hee-hee! Ah, childhood..."

He breathed a sigh of relief that Tim, this young American entrepreneur he'd never met before, survived that ordeal. But now this conversation was starting to catch Maou's curiosity.

"Egypt, Hawaii, Indonesia... Where did I last hear those...?"

"I, uh, I feel like we should've banished those from our memories forever, dude..."

It had obviously sent Ashiya's and Urushihara's antennae up as well, but it was Suzuno who reached the right conclusion first.

"Hawaii, Indonesia, Egypt—Ms. Shiba's sent us letters and photos from all those places, hasn't she?"

""""Whoooaaaaaahhhhhhhh!!""""

The simple observation conjured up traumatic memories in the minds of all three demons—a Pandora's box, sealed away and never to be discussed again. The peacock festooned in gold, the belly dancer undulating in front of the pyramids—and in another moment, the Devil King and his two generals recalled the one photo. The photo to end all photos. The *swimsuit* shot.

"E-excuse me! I need a breath of fresh air! Frggh…!"

Ashiya bounded out of the room.

"Ngggggghhhhhhh…!"

With a groan not from this world, Urushihara fell back into bed, the color seeming to escape his eyes, skin, and the rest of him. It was a perfect match with his hair as he lay there, desiccating, while the machine Acieth messed around with began emitting ominous *beep*s and *boop*s.

"Nn…nn…gh! I…I can beat this…!"

A waterfall of sweat ran down Maou's face as he fought off the horror.

"What is it, Devil King?"

"Oh? Do you need to go to the bathroom, Devil King?"

"What has gotten into them?" Nord asked. "I don't know," Laila listlessly replied.

Maou glared down hard upon his landlord, even as the forbidden, hideous, now-legendary photograph weighed deeply upon his mind.

"You… You guys… You knew about us from the start…"

Shiba nodded. "Well, ever since the whole Laila affair, you could say that our family's been keeping our eyes peeled for Gates opening and closing around here. We were not awaiting your arrival in particular, Mr. Maou—rather, following Laila, we were simply expecting another visitor from Ente Isla. Laila was our only source for information on events in Ente Isla, and what she said indicated that whatever was pursuing her couldn't be very good for Earth, now could it?"

She wound up waiting another fifteen years for Nord, the next visitor, to arrive, followed in relatively short time by Maou, Ashiya, and Emi.

"We knew that Nord would be following Laila's trail to this planet, and while it may be rude of me to put it this way, we knew that Ms. Yusa would be something of a lower priority. Compared to her, you demons were much more of a threat to Earth and its citizens. Not to discount what Laila told us, of course, but as strong as she was, she didn't pose a direct danger the way that you potentially did. And so all of us in the Earth Sephirah family decided that, if Nord and Ms. Yusa aren't here to cause trouble, we had best avoid contact with them as much as possible."

"Really?" Suzuno interjected. At this point, it was clear that Shiba already knew everything Laila was involved with, as well as the Yesod fragments and perhaps even the Tree of Sephirot itself, birthplace of all Sephirah. "Even though Emilia already had the holy sword...or the Yesod fragment, I should say?"

Shiba gave a firm nod. "It may not have looked like it does now, but Ms. Yusa was already serving as the 'latent force' or whatnot to that holy sword. Once that happened, you couldn't take the fragment out of her unless the fragment *wanted* out."

This made sense. Emi was deemed harmless enough by Shiba's family, despite being a stranger from a very strange land. And despite draining her holy energy and having her angelic side all but taken away by Sariel's Evil Eye of the Fallen attack, Emi's holy sword had never left her.

"The only way to remove a Sephirah from its latent force is if the force itself dies, the Sephirah leaves of its own free will, or we take a certain final measure—a measure that, judging by the state of Ente Isla, isn't available right now. That is why we decided that focusing on Ms. Yusa could wait for a less hectic time."

"All right. May I ask one more thing?"

"Yes?" she replied to Suzuno.

"You said your family preferred to remain uninvolved if these 'visitors' were not a threat to Earth. But what about *that*?"

"H-hey, I'm not 'that,' Suzuno. Quit pointing at me!"

"The Devil King is the Devil King. The sworn enemy of all mankind. I expect he would be far more harmful to Earth than— *Oww!*"

"Hold it, Suzuno," Maou said as he grabbed Suzuno's bundled hair and pulled. "I ain't gonna let that slide. I'm worse for Earth than the angels?"

"Wh-what are you...?!"

The normally meek cleric found herself pulled into the air, flailing her limbs like a crab at the fish market.

"That," Shiba replied, "was why I paid *personal* attention to you and Ashiya when you arrived."

"Huh?"

"What? Agh! Let me go, Devil King!!"

"I could tell immediately that you housed a tremendously dangerous force within yourselves. You may have lost your negative demonic force, but you still posed the threat of unspeakable brutality upon us all. So I watched you for a while, and if you made any untoward moves at all, I intended to wipe you off the planet."

"Uh?"

Maou searched for Ashiya, before remembering he had fled the room earlier.

"But luckily for all of us, my concerns turned out to be over nothing!"

"S-so you are saying this Devil King was not a brutal threat to us at all? I *said*, let me *go*, you fiend...!"

"Well, goodness me, I never dreamed for a moment that their first priority would be to get their ID papers in order and search for an apartment! Not even Laila demonstrated such eagerness to join human society. And they never used that demonic force at all—not even when Mr. Maou went to the hospital with malnutrition after not eating for three days. Instead, he wrote up a résumé and started applying for work, right on the spot. Hardly dangerous behavior, I thought."

Which all meant that, from the moment Maou reached Japan

until he met Emi and defeated Urushihara, Shiba was always watching them.

"Malnutrition?"

"Sh-shut up!"

This was also the first time Suzuno heard anything about the demons' lives on Earth before she showed up. She gave him a doubtful look. "Ugh," she groaned as she attempted to fix her rumpled hair with her hands. "What are you going to do if this hair is permanently damaged, hmm?"

"Uh, don't tell me the management company was all run by Sephirah dudes, too…?"

Maou recalled the property management company he and Ashiya called upon several times while Shiba was abroad. Shiba shook her head lightly in response.

"For that, I simply registered Villa Rosa Sasazuka with all the nearby rental management firms, once I could guess where you were settling down. It took quite a bit of money, mind you, given the suddenness of my requests, but…well, I have my hand in quite a number of businesses, so they all came to an agreement, of course."

He didn't want to know more about any of these businesses, but even by ex-Sephirah standards, all this discussion about Shiba's financial and family situation indicated to Maou that her bank account was probably on a far higher plane of existence than his.

"I then turned my observations to your neighbors, everyone at MgRonald, Chiho Sasaki, Ms. Yusa, and so forth. Seeing you interact with them, I concluded that as long as you were in a stable living situation, you were not only perfectly harmless; you would even eliminate any other potential threats from other worlds! Having to repair the damage done to my apartment gave me quite a fright, I have to say to you, but thank heavens Ohguro-ya was willing to take you on."

Maou's face twisted in discomfort. He had been dancing in the palm of the Sephirah from the very beginning.

When Shiba sent that video referring the demons to the Ohguro-ya restaurant and sundry shop on the beaches of Chiba, Maou had left it unwatched for days, too afraid of what it may contain. But he should have realized it—when he finally called Amane, she gave no indication the place was hiring anyone *besides* Maou and his companions. It was the first warning sign for what wound up being an extremely abnormal few days.

"So that's it, huh? I can't say I like it much," Maou said as he confronted his landlord. He had spent much of this year fighting off a number of otherworldly invaders, from Sariel onward, mainly to protect his own daily routine. If that was all Shiba had been doing from the start, it certainly felt like he was being taken advantage of.

"You've been using me this whole time, just so life would be easier for you guys?"

"By that," Shiba replied coolly, "do you mean to say you didn't choose to protect Japan and your current lifestyle of your own free will?"

"...No, not that, but..."

"Because I made the choice to trust in you and Ashiya as regular human beings. And you've always so wonderfully lived up to that trust!"

"Well, not that I need to hear that from you or anything, but I kinda like it here. Japan, and Earth. I can't live like I am right now forever, but it's a pretty chill place, I think. But that's why..."

His gaze darted between Laila and Shiba as he collected his thoughts.

"Like, what are you people *after*? You wanna talk about that, right? And lemme just tell you guys, I'm not in a good mood about this right now."

"Of—of course I do," Laila said, looking up with pleading eyes. "I've been waiting for this moment for so long! Waiting for people as strong as you and Emilia to appear at the same time..."

There was no longer anything divine in those eyes, none of the soothing guidance she gave Maou once upon a time. The swollen cheeks made pulling off a "divine" expression a pretty tall order, but even beyond that, it was clear this was an angel at the end of her rope. Was it being so thoroughly rejected by her daughter that brought her there, or…?

"We…we need your powers…to save the world… To save Ente—"

It was a clumsy request. And ironically, it made Maou immediately lose interest in everything he wanted to know about Laila's true intentions.

"Stop."

Laila blinked at the sudden about-face in Maou's request.

"Ms. Shiba?"

"Yes?"

"Urushihara's healthy enough to leave, right? Is his hair ever gonna go back to normal?"

The color had left a lot more than just Urushihara's hair, he could now see, as he breezily changed the subject.

"Um…wait… Satan?"

"Oh, definitely so, once he is away from my side."

The logic of this didn't quite make sense, but Maou accepted it.

"I'm heading out, too. And I'd appreciate it if you brought Urushihara home ASAP, too, you guys."

"Wh-what? Sa-Satan?"

"Devil King… You…"

"Oh, oh? Is it over? If we are going home, maybe we eat the lunch? At the restaurant?"

"W-wait!!" Laila shouted over Suzuno and Acieth. She stood up, attempting to take Maou by the hand. He easily dodged it.

"Sa-Satan?"

"I'm not interested in listening anymore. This has been exhausting, so I'm going home. I've got work tomorrow."

"Wait. Wait! What is the meaning of this?! This has everything to do with you demons, too!"

"Yeah, I'll bet it does. But judging from everything you guys told me, it's not a 'world' danger so much as a, like, danger to people on Ente Isla, yeah? Not really something we demons need to lose sleep over."

"N-no, you're wrong! You're all just as…!"

"Don't you get it?! I'm not *interested*!!"

The shout shook the walls of the room, sending Laila reeling back like someone had shot her.

"Satan… Why?"

Ignoring the saddened angel, Maou staggered toward the door, hints of *that photo* still lingering in his mind. Suzuno followed, bewildered, and so did Acieth, who didn't look like she was thinking about much of anything.

"If I felt like it, I could beat the shit out of anything up to and including Gabriel right now, okay? Feel free to visit Nord all you want, but don't you dare go up the stairs to my place."

He placed a hand on the door handle, then turned to Laila.

"See you."

The door creaked shut behind him.

"Wait! D-Devil King, wait! …Agh! Alciel! What happened?!"

Hurriedly following behind, Suzuno found herself yelping as she went through the doorway.

"Wowww," the dubious Acieth added.

"Acieth!" came a voice from Nord, behind her.

"Oooh, um, sorry, Dad," she muttered.

"I know. I know you aren't here because you want to be."

"No, I am, Dad," she replied, cutting him off. "I, um, I really hated all the things, in beginning, but now, I like. And everybody, too, I like."

She turned to the others. It was unclear whether "everybody" included Urushihara, now thoroughly withered after she played doctor with the machines next to him, but she still gave a sad shake of her head.

"I know what Maou says, what Chiho says, what Emi feels. Mom, I don't hate, but, mmm, I think, maybe Mom could do something a little quicker, before now? It is complicated."

"Acieth…"

"And sorry, Mom, but I want to go with Maou and rest. For the little while longer."

"Acieth? But you're..."

"I know. I know it. I will not do the stupid things. But...your side, Mom, I cannot be right now. You are...angel, too, Mom."

"...!!"

Acieth turned to Shiba. "Mikitty?"

"Yes?"

"I—I am 'single' right now, yes? You did something, before?"

"...Yes. The 'final measure.'" The landlord paused, a rarity for her. "I felt, over on Ente Isla, that the influence of Mr. Maou's demonic force was starting to point you in the, shall we way, wrong direction."

"You know, maybe I not think a lot first, but Maou is host I chose. Mikitty, you do not have the say in this."

"...No, I suppose not. I apologize for my impertinence."

"So you, Mikitty, take care of own Yesod. I..." She whirled around. "I going back to Maou." Then she was off.

Each one of them, for reasons of their own, left Laila behind them, one by one. All that was left was Shiba, Amane, Nord, the increasingly leathery Urushihara, and Laila.

"Why...?"

The plaintive voice failed to reach Maou, who was too busy carrying Ashiya (whom they had found twitching in the hospital corridor) to notice as Acieth caught up to them all waiting for the elevator.

✻

Maou didn't hear much of anything about what Chiho and Emeralda did or talked about as they pursued Emi. On the surface, both Chiho and Emi seemed calm—or at least, willing to pretend that day in Urushihara's hospital room hadn't happened—as they went on with their lives, so it didn't seem right to rehash the topic. As Ashiya put it, Nord and Laila apparently paid several visits to Eifukucho, but judging by the way Emi was acting, he doubted she gave them the time of day.

So, pedaling the Dullahan II, he made his way home as always and climbed up their creaky stairway as always. The light was on in Nord's place downstairs, but he didn't care to check whether anyone was inside.

Through the door, he was greeted by Ashiya's dinner and Urushihara's back. A normal day, in other words, in the tiny Devil's Castle he had built for himself in Japan. For now, that was enough. But tonight, an extraneous element or two was in the mix.

"Why are *you* here so late?"

Suzuno was waiting for him.

"Laila visited today. With Ms. Shiba and Gabriel."

"Oh? Huh," he distractedly replied. "What's for dinner tonight, Ashiya?"

"Some deep-fried tofu and miso soup for now, sir. I could prepare some tofu steaks from the freezer if you'd like something else."

"Nah. I got all my break time in today, so I should keep it light."

"Very well, my liege. I will reheat it in just a moment."

"I imagined you had no interest in listening to them, so I tried to send them away, but…"

"So why are you here?"

"I…" Suzuno's face reddened for a moment, for some inexplicable reason. Then, recalling her errand, she recomposed herself. "Listening to them…I am starting to feel they are winning me over."

"Big whoop. You're a Church cleric. She's an angel, you know."

"That… Well, yes, but… Listen. On the other hand, I mean…"

Her face reddened a tad once more. Then, finally summoning the willpower, she slapped a hand on the table in the center of room, just as Ashiya was laying out dinner.

"Why do you so steadfastly refuse to hear Laila out?!"

"Hey, think of the time. They'll hear you downstairs."

"Nh… What is with all this…?"

For all they knew, Laila might have been downstairs with Nord. Nobody was sure where Laila called home, exactly, but it was definitely somewhere around the greater Shinjuku area, and thus an easy train ride away. Maou clearly had a cruel streak toward her, but now here he was, looking out for his neighbors. She wanted to talk to him; he didn't want to hear; but they were separated only by a tatami-mat floor, a baseboard, and the ceiling down below, and those were no obstacles by their standards.

"You make no sense," she sighed, balling up her hands as she knelt.

"Look, what I said before is the whole thing. I really don't care about her story. But can't you kind of picture what's at the end of it?"

"The end of it?"

"You know what she wants. She wants me, Emi—you too, of course, and Emeralda, and Ashiya and Urushihara, and maybe Amane and Albert in the mix, too—she wants us to all band together and save Ente Isla from some horrible threat looming over it. What kinda threat, I don't know."

"Mmm… Yes, certainly."

"Whatever this threat is, it's gonna involve Alas Ramus, Acieth, and Erone on a super-deep level, and we're gonna have to do something about this planet's Sephirah and stuff, yeah? And since me and Emi are 'latent forces'—which I *still* wanna know what that means, by the way—we can't stay uninvolved, either. So like, do I really need it spelled out for me any further?"

"…If you want a simple yes or no answer to that, then from my perspective, yes, we do."

"And from *my* perspective," Maou countered with a smile, "the answer's never gonna be anything but a no."

"…"

"Your dinner, my liege."

Urushihara did not budge an inch from his computer.

"I mean, remember, if every man, woman, and child were wiped off the surface of Ente Isla, then everything's comin' up roses, as far as we're concerned. If my landlord's telling the truth, then all we gotta do is wait a few more centuries, right? Humans would be useful to me if I'm ruling over 'em, maybe, but it's gonna be hard to fight any more over there than we have already, not to mention a royal pain in the ass to organize. If you asked me, I'd like to see Ente Isla destroyed more than *not* destroyed. Oh, thanks, Ashiya."

Suzuno remained silent, watching Maou suspiciously as he tucked in. He didn't seem to be putting on a show. On paper, it was an incredibly cruel thing to say, if regrettably expectable from the Devil King. But Suzuno already knew what he *really* was, inside. And that "real" person, the one not bound by names like Satan or Sadao Maou, didn't mean any of it literally. There was some other intention behind those words.

She decided to wait for him to continue, staring intently as he sipped his soup, huffed in surprise at how hot the tofu was, and filled up his bowl of rice two more times.

"...You sure are stubborn, aren't you?"

"It is a trait of mine."

"You aren't getting anything else."

"You are not a liar, but you are not an honest man, either. I know that just as well as everyone else."

"Yeah, thanks a lot. Can you just go? It's gotta be a cardinal sin for a woman like you to stay in a house full of men this late."

"I care not. A bit too late to change my ways now."

"...I'd love to hear what Chiho Sasaki would say if she heard that," Urushihara chimed in. "You don't care about what, exactly?"

"Enough of that! You know how strange Bell has been acting lately."

Maou sighed at the two men whispering behind him. "I don't," he finally said, borrowing a line from Kawata, "wanna be on the hook for someone else's life."

"You what?"

"Plus, whether I've got an obligation to save all the Ente Islans or listen to Laila or not—no matter what she tried to push on me back there, I still have no reason to take action."

Suzuno remained silent once more, weighing each word carefully.

"You can stare at me all you want, Suzuno; that's all I got for you. Like, seriously, that's the only reason."

"…I suppose it is." She stared for a few moments more, then stood up, resigning herself to defeat. "Then I wonder why I am even here."

"Not because anybody needs to see *me*, I'll tell you that."

"You saw how Emilia and Chiho were. They are my friends, and if *this* is how they and the angel I suppose I am bound to serve wish to act, then I want to conform to that. My skills are not particularly useful in any other field, after all. I would also like to keep my potential second career as a Great Demon General on the back burner, just in case."

"Kind of a blasphemous thing for a cleric to say, isn't it?"

"Thank you for your time."

With an ironic smile, she put her sandals on, preparing to leave Room 201. But she was stopped by a totally unexpected question behind her:

"Suzuno, do you know anything about metallurgy?"

"Metal— What?" she said, raising an eyebrow. "You mean, blacksmithing and the like?"

"Yeah. I never even touched any iron weapons until just after the Devil King's Army started up."

"And?"

"Well, iron's played a huge role in the history of civilization, right? Way stronger than stone or copper. Strong enough to turn ancient society on its side, and all that."

"Yes…?"

Suzuno stood by the door, unsure where this was going. The major nations of Ente Isla got their start by mastering the art of forging iron, just as the Hittites did back in the fifteenth century BCE on Earth. But how did this connect to anything they were talking about?

"Thing is, though, the idea of preventative maintenance hadn't really taken hold much in the demon realm. We wasted a lot of good iron weaponry, thanks to the way we abused them."

"Yes, and what is the point of this?" Suzuno snapped back, annoyed at the mystery tangent.

"Oh, nothing. It just came to mind, is all. Sorry."

"Ugh. You make no sense to me."

"No, I just mean, y'know, maintenance is important. I'm gonna be driving a scooter around again, once delivery starts up, so I just thought about it. 'Course, what I did to that bike on Ente Isla goes a little beyond what a regular check-up can handle, but…"

The two Honta Gyro-Roof scooters Suzuno provided for their quest on Ente Isla, which played a major role in getting Emi back to Japan safely, still weren't back here. They were pretty well wrecked in Heavensky, capital of the planet's Eastern Island, after what Maou and Acieth did to them. Albert promised he'd recover all the parts that fell off and ferry them back safely, but that hadn't happened yet. Given the wholly alien make of those bikes, Maou doubted whether Albert would know what a bike part looked like if he even saw one—but it's not like he and Suzuno were any hurry to run an errand back to Heavensky for them.

"…Anyway, we're gonna be pretty short-staffed on the delivery front. And if Laila's here, there's no need to run bodyguard duty for Nord any longer, yeah? So why don't you apply to MgRonald, too?"

"I'll pass, thank you. I am not in the habit of smiling at people for the sake of politeness. Scowling, on the other hand…"

"That's just a waste of talent, dude," Urushihara cut in.

"……………I would be rather happier if a human said that to me," she sniped back.

"Ooh, you look pretty happy to hear it anyway, I'd say—"

"Enough!" Ashiya shouted.

"F-farewell to you!" Suzuno shouted at equal volume as she hurried herself out the door. Maou couldn't help but chuckle as she left.

"You know," he said as he turned toward his roommates, "we've got nothing urgent going on right now. I'd say our top priority should be to retain our current lifestyle in Japan and, you know, try to upgrade it a little. Right?"

"Absolutely, Your Demonic Highness."

Ashiya nodded deeply, even though the proposal sounded a bit off to him. Urushihara, meanwhile, just sighed at what, to him, seemed like an unnatural affinity for stagnation on top of stagnation.

"It's all just 'don't rock the boat, don't rock the boat' with you guys, huh? Well, if that's what you want, take it, I guess…"

THE HERO STARTS LOOKING FOR A NEW PATH

On her way home from school after wrapping up her extracurricular activities, Chiho was greeted with an unfamiliar phone number on her screen. She waited for it to vibrate a few times before picking it up.

"Hello…?"

"Oh, hellooo, is this Sasakiii?"

"Oh, Emeralda! Wow! What's up?"

She had no idea Emeralda had her own phone. *Better save the number,* she thought before her friend continued.

"Listen, sorry for calling so suuuddenly, but I wanted to aaask you something."

"Sure."

"Do you knowww where Emilia is right nowww?"

"…Emilia?"

Chiho stopped walking.

"She hasn't been back hooome, not since two days after we all met Lailaaa at the hospital."

"She hasn't? Huh?" She was having trouble parsing this. "She's left the place empty?"

"She hasn't been baaack, no. She said she was going to work, but now it's been three whole daaays…"

"Wait a second! Yusa's been working shifts at MgRonald the past three days in a row, you know!"

"*Oh?*"

A light gasp made its way through the phone line.

"Yeah, we've been talking like normal and everything...and we've been walking to Sasazuka station together after our shifts. She's taking the train *somewhere*."

"*R-reeeeally? Oh, oh my gosssh...!*"

This was apparently not the response Emeralda was expecting.

"I heard that Nord and Suzuno tried visiting Yusa's place earlier, with Laila in tow. Was she gone then, too?"

"*Oh, that would've been when she left work in the eeevening, or was meant to. But she never went hooome...*"

"So even at that point..." Chiho recalled that day just before Urushihara left the hospital, when she brought some food over to Villa Rosa Sasazuka only to find no one there. "Have you tried calling her? This is your phone you're using, right?"

"*Yes, Emilia made Al and me purchase these when we first visited Japaaan. I did try calling, but she never annnswered... Is she scheduled for work todaaay?*"

"Um, give me just a moment."

Still unsure what was going on, Chiho took out a notebook with the next two weeks' worth of shifts on it and gave it a quick scan.

"Oh, she's off today."

"*Ohhh,*" Emeralda groaned, at a total loss. There was no way to track her movements today.

What's gotten into her? Leaving her home in Eifukucho empty, without even contacting the friend she trusts the most?

If Emeralda was telling the truth, this bizarre behavior must have been related to Laila somehow—but if so, there was no reason to leave without a word. If Emi didn't want to see her mother, there were a thousand more natural ways to go about it, given her personality—shut the door on her, tell Emeralda to shoo her away, whatever.

It made Chiho recall what happened when she followed her out of the hospital room.

✳

"I—I don't see herrr. Where did she gooo…?"

"Over here!"

Once they were outside the hospital, Emeralda swiveled her head around in search of Emi, as Chiho followed her phone down the path to Yoyogi Park.

"H-how do you know she's there? Do you think she's going to board one of those traaains?"

"I don't know, but I'm sure she's headed toward the station… Ah?!"

She let out a little shout just as she finished running up the path leading to JR Yoyogi station.

"It's going faster… Maybe she got in a taxi."

Emeralda gave her a surprised stare. Chiho didn't acknowledge it, too busy staring into the distance as she clutched her phone.

"From the intersection in front of the station… She's probably going that way," she said, pointing down a street neatly running between two lines of tall buildings. "But where's she going? Back to Eifukucho? Is that the right direction?"

She was tracking Emi's movements, somehow—it seemed like magic to Emeralda—but still didn't know where she was headed.

"Oh, no, she's too far. It's going all over the place." Heaving a great sigh, she stopped, putting her phone away. "…I think Yusa's taking a taxi back home, Emeralda. You're staying with her, right?"

"Y-yesss… But how did you do that, Ms. Sasakiii? Did you have a gut feeeeling about her?"

Chiho showed Emeralda her pink mobile phone, flashing an embarrassed little smile. "I have an Idea Link running through this. I'm only supposed to use it for emergencies, but…"

"An Idea Link?!"

The news almost made Emeralda leap into the air.

"I was beaming a signal to Yusa's phone as I was running, but she's too far away for me to track at this point…"

"M-Ms. Sasakiii, when did you learn how to use an Idea Link?! And how?! You're from Japaaan, aren't you?!"

The extent of her shock was clear in her speech.

"Well, Yusa and Suzuno, and Sariel, too…they taught me a bunch of stuff and I learned how to do it."

"Sariel?! Sariel the archangel?! The one who took a job nearby Emilia and the Devil King and tried to capture her?! What has been *happening* over here?!"

She had reason to be alarmed. First, Chiho, a girl with no latent holy force, had mastered a magic that ran on just that type of force. Second, it was impossible for her to imagine a situation where Emi and Suzuno would team up with Sariel, of all people, to make that so.

"Well," Chiho bashfully explained, "a lot of stuff happened before Yusa was captured in Ente Isla. The angels and demons kinda came to realize that I'm the weak link when it comes to Maou and Yusa, so I asked them to teach me, just in case there was some urgent danger and I needed to call them."

"Ohhh," Emeralda said, finally recovering from the initial shock. "But my, how amaaazing. Amazing resolve, and amazing abilllity, too. An Idea Link is high-level maaagic! One would normally spend a year at the academy mastering it."

Chiho gave a polite, bashful smile at the outspoken praise. "Enough about me, though," she said, darkening once more. "We need to think about Yusa. I think she's back home by now. Let's hurry."

"B-buuut what should we say to herrr…?"

"Let's worry about that once we find her!"

She grabbed Emeralda's hand and made a beeline for the station. Calling a taxi was something neither the teenage girl nor the Ente Islan sorceress had ever done before, so she decided to play it safe with the train.

"M-Ms. Sasakiii, have you chaaanged a little since last we met?"

Emeralda couldn't help but smile, somehow, as she was dragged along. She recalled her first visit to Japan, when Chiho was caught up in all the Ente Isla chaos—such an innocent young girl, troubled over how much distance she should take from her crush. Now, the girl dragging her ahead had no doubts plaguing her mind.

"I have to keep strong inside, at least," she said between breaths, "or else I'll never keep up with Maou and Yusa!"

And she was. Emeralda could feel the strength, the hope within her. It made her think aloud:

"…I am so happy you've become friends with Emeralda…"

"What?"

"Oh, nothiiing. Can we duck into that alleyway, Ms. Sasakiii?"

"Huh? That one?"

"Yesss, I just remembered a shorrrtcut…"

This shortcut was news to the confused Chiho, but she still turned them into a side street, too narrow for more than one car to pass at once. And just as they disappeared from the main boulevard they were on:

"Hyaaaaaaaaaaaaaaaaaahhhhhhhhh…"

The surprised scream from Chiho echoed its way upward, far past the tall buildings of Yoyogi.

✳

Emi had, as Chiho surmised, returned to Eifukucho. She was still in a state of shock about her and Laila—but not enough so to keep her from lecturing Emeralda about literally flying into her apartment from the sky with Chiho.

This was part of the reason, by the way, why Chiho didn't realize until she was on her way home that it was her first visit to Emi's place. She had always wanted to see how Emi lived, what kind of setup she had here—but Emi acted so eerily normal, so perfectly like herself, that this fact didn't occur to her until long after. Just because everything was hunky-dory on the outside didn't mean she was okay on the inside, of course. But really, it was the same-old, same-old with her, even at work the next day. That made

Chiho put her guard down, and now they had no idea where she was. Great.

Given Emi's personality and her current situation, Chiho doubted she was staying at some cheap hotel or camping out at an Internet café. That left only a few possibilities. She studied the shift schedule for a few moments, then nodded.

"…There's a potential lead I want to check out. Can you give me a little while?"

"*All riiight,*" the depressed Emeralda replied to close out the call. "*Thank youuu!*"

Then, without giving it much further deep thought, Chiho looked up a phone number from her list and called it.

"Oh, hello, this is Sasaki. Um, so I guess Yusa hasn't been—"

"*Gehhh!!*"

Even before she could state her business, the voice on the other end let out a surprised squeal of terror. Chiho had inadvertently painted her right into a corner.

"…Well, judging by that, Ms. Suzuki, it sounds like you know where she is?"

She could almost hear Rika Suzuki hesitating on the other end of the line.

As her former coworker, Rika was now caught up in Ente Isla events in much the same vein as Chiho, having a fairly firm grasp about who Maou and Emi really were. She gave Emi a lot of mental support, and if Emi was anywhere, Chiho reasoned, it was almost certainly her place.

"*Yeah, I guess I do, Chiho,*" she admitted. "*But could you, like, wait 'til tomorrow for me, maybe?*"

This struck Chiho as odd. It suggested maybe Emi wasn't with Rika after all.

"…Well, that's okay by me, but it's not good for her to do that without saying anything to Emeralda. Maybe they're such close friends that it's hard for her to talk about it 'n' stuff, but… Like, you know how it feels weird to open up your friend's refrigerator for something, even if they say it's okay? It's like that."

"Ha-ha-ha!"

The laugh sounded a bit strained to Chiho.

"Yeah, I guess it's been pretty rough for Emeralda. Emi's been telling me a lot... I guess she's been through some bad stuff again, huh? They finally found her mom, too."

"Or whatever you wanna call it, yeah," she replied, fully expecting that Emi had provided Rika most of the details.

"So I figure I know most of the story now, but, y'know, if I can be honest with ya, we can't dance around it like this forever, I don't think. We're gonna have to all face up to it and really do something, at some point."

Chiho knew that as well. Laila certainly made a dramatic entrance, but not one that necessarily foretold major changes in Emi's and Maou's lives. Maybe she'd reveal why she was skulking around for so long and put out those smoldering doubts in their minds, but that was about it. And she knew it probably involved Laila having some major mission under way, one she wanted Emi's and Maou's strength on her side for.

It's just...

"But I mean, it's not like Emi's in any big rush right now, yeah?"

Rika had it right on the nose.

Emi's ultimate mission was to slay Maou, Ashiya, and Urushihara, but—thankfully for Chiho—it was becoming more and more unclear just how serious she was about that. She had recovered her long-lost father, and she returned the favor she owed Maou for saving her from Olba's clutches. The Malebranche forces that rose up after Satan's defeat on the Eastern Island were loyal to him once more, and both Shiba and Gabriel claimed that the heavens, after an extended period of meddling, no longer wanted anything to do with planet Earth.

Now, Sariel was interested in nothing but his rose-tinged future with Mayumi Kisaki, and Gabriel was thoroughly cowed by the powers of Shiba, Amane, and Maou surrounding him. Emi even had a new job to sustain her, here in Japan.

To Emi, the big mission right now, if there was one, was to have fun and make something out of the days she spent on this planet. The lack of any clear and present enemy didn't mean she was out of the forest, going forward, but she *did* have a network of friends to rely on, a veritable lineup of powerful fighters to swiftly step up should things go awry. If anything, she was safe to retire from battle for good and go back to wheat farming with her father, although Maou's presence was the main reason why she hadn't. Maou demonstrated zero interest in leaving Japan, and thus Emi's hands were tied.

"...Hmm."

"Whatcha thinking, Chiho?"

"Oh, um, nothing, exactly..."

Going over Emi's situation in her mind, Chiho discovered something that confused her. Emi's old mission, to slay the Devil King, was just a shell of what it once was—but it had never wholly disappeared. That was because the Devil King's Army that Maou had led had caused so much pain not just to her, but to countless Ente Islans, and Emi still felt he had to be judged for that. But Emi's hostility toward Maou had absolutely mellowed compared to before. In fact, it almost seemed like things were drifting toward exactly what Chiho wanted—all her friends, living together, being happy.

After distilling all this down, however, only one simple conclusion was left: Emi was stuck in Japan because of Maou. The thought severely unnerved Chiho.

"Yeah, I'm sure you've got mixed feelings about all this, too, huh, Chiho? I mean, she hasn't come out and said it, but I'm getting little hints that Emi doesn't really hate Maou the way she used to."

"Th-that's fine! I mean, I like it that way!"

She blushed, even though nobody was there to see it. She had forgotten about Rika's incredible intuition, as well as her deep interest in friendship drama. If she knew that much, Emi must have been pretty frank with her feelings when they spoke.

"Hee-hee! Well, when it comes to that *sorta thing, I think you oughtta just follow your heart, y'know?"*

"What do you mean, 'that sort of thing'?"

If Rika was here right now, she thought, *she'd probably be laughing at how mad I look.*

"Aww, you knowww! So basically, Emi's pretty much filed away any desire to whip Maou's ass for now, right? Or rather, it feels like that goal of hers has gotten a lot more vague."

"Y-yeah, more or less."

"And having this hell-raiser of a mom pop in just when things are chilling out a little? Yeah, I'd be mad, too. Even though none of it is Emi's responsibility, it's like this mom she's never even met just returns all of a sudden from some place after piling up debt then putting Emi on the hook for it, y'know? She doesn't have to put up with that."

It was kind of a blunt analogy, but it made a lot of sense.

"So, you know, I'm trying to be a good friend for her to vent at 'n' all, but since I know all about what's going on with these guys, I can't help but see things Emeralda's way a little more. I mean, she's super-strong in a lot of ways, I know, so I guess part of me thinks that she could really pitch in with this."

"Oh, yeah, um... I guess so."

"And I talked about getting put on the hook just now, but Emi's mom isn't, like, totally evil, right? Not like Olba or those angels. I bet she's just like, 'come on, you're the Hero, we need your strength to save the world and stuff.'"

"I think you're exactly right." Chiho nodded, recalling what Shiba had told her.

"But the thing is, Emi's in no shape to take that up right now, and she doesn't have any duty to, either."

"Yeah."

"So that's why I think, like, not in terms of work or whatever, but I think Emi should try keeping herself busy with something that's really important to her life."

"Keep herself busy?"

It was a little too roundabout for Chiho to follow. But Rika laughed it off, expecting it.

"Hey, do you have some free time right now, Chiho?"

"Huh? Oh, um, yeah, I don't have work today, so..."

"Okay, well, I'll text Emi once I'm off the line with you, so why don't you try runnin' over to her? I think it'd be the perfect time for you to catch up, where she is, and it's gonna be a lot of fun."

"Umm, sure, but the perfect time how? And over where?"

"Yeah, you'll see what I mean. You're, um, seventeen, right?"

"Uh-huh…"

What's my age got to do with it?

"Emi ain't going anywhere, so you can take your time headin' over. Just wait, like, half a day before telling Emeralda, okay? Like, contact her after you see Emi. Sound good? I'll go text her now."

"Um, sure, thanks a…"

Rika hung up before Chiho could finish. Thirty seconds later, she texted her.

"That was fast!"

Must've had one composed in advance for when I called her, she thought. But the message only perplexed her further.

"…Where's that?"

It looked like a residential address. Sticking it into her map application, Chiho saw it was a fourth-floor apartment nearby Zoshigaya Station, in the Toshima ward of north-central Tokyo. From Sasazuka, it'd involve taking the Toei-Shinjuku Line to Shinjuku-sanchome Station, then changing to the Tokyo Metro Fukutoshin subway line—about a forty-five-minute journey in all.

The name that accompanied Rika's text, though, was unfamiliar to Chiho.

"Maki Shimizu…?"

"Is this it?"

It was just before six PM, and given the date on the calendar, the sun was already most of the way down by the time Chiho stopped by a small concrete building nestled between Zoshigaya Station and the tram stop serving the nearby Kishiboshin Temple.

"Comfort Building, Room 401. Guess so."

She nervously checked the address against the building's name multiple times before pushing the button by the autolock doors. None of the residential mailboxes had names on them to refer to.

"Hello!" came the crackly, unfamiliar voice of a woman.

"Um, is this the Shimizu residence?"

"That's right. Who's this?"

The voice sounded a tad suspicious—Chiho knew she didn't sound too confident.

"Umm, my name's Sasaki. Rika Suzuki told me that Emi Yusa might be—"

"Oh! Ohhhhh."

Rika's name unlocked the padlock in the woman's mind. Her voice ratcheted up.

"Right, right, right, right, right, I heard about you! Hey, boss! I'll buzz you in now! Hey, Yusa, Sasaki's here to see you!"

Click.

"Ah…"

She seemed awfully worked up about something before hanging up, but the doors whirred open anyway.

"'Boss'?"

This was increasingly not what she was expecting. It bewildered her. Emi was definitely there, but she still had no idea who this Shimizu girl was. She took the elevator to the fourth floor; the door she wanted was waiting just beyond. There wasn't any name card anywhere—maybe to prevent crime, or something.

Taking another deep breath, Chiho pushed the doorbell button. "Welcome, welcome!" came the immediate response, as if they were waiting to ambush her. The door opened, revealing a woman slightly older than Chiho beaming from ear to ear.

"Yow! Hey, boss! Aww, you're just cute as a button, aren't ya? Just like Rika said!"

"Oh, um, hi. My name's Chiho Sasaki."

"Great to meet you! C'mon in. Hey, Yusa! Your cute li'l gal's here!"

"Um, ummmmm," Chiho murmured as she was sucked into the

room, as if the tenant had just turned on a huge vacuum cleaner. Then:

"Oh!"

"Hey. Sorry I made you worry."

"Hi, Chi-Sis!"

In the room immediately past the door, Chiho's eyes turned to Emi, looking at her a bit awkwardly from the sofa, and Alas Ramus, chilling out next to her and playing with a teddy bear.

"Yusa!" Chiho shouted, keeping up her brisk jog into the room. "You really scared me! Emeralda said you've been gone for a while! I didn't notice anything different at work, so..."

"Yeah, sorry about that. I guess I kind of lost my head."

It was a very non-Emi-like excuse, but given how she stuck to her work schedule, she must have made the decision with a rational mind. Exactly why she felt it necessary to worry Emeralda so much was still an enigma, but Chiho breathed a sigh of relief anyway.

"Whew... I mean, me and Maou weren't too worried, but you should really say something to Emeralda, at least. It's not like she doesn't know what you're going through."

"Yeah. I do feel bad about that," she meekly admitted, her face turned down. "I'll apologize to her when I get home."

It was a relief to Chiho just to know that Emi wasn't in serious trouble. But why was she here? And who's this Maki Shimizu? The questions piled up. Spotting the concern on her face, Emi pointed behind the girl.

"Oh, um, Maki Shimizu over there's an old coworker from my Dokodemo days."

"Hi!" Maki chirped.

"Hi!" Alas Ramus shouted out in glee alongside her.

"Yusa helped me out all the time at work! She really did!"

"Did she...?" Chiho asked, practically overwhelmed by her bright, vigorous energy. Rika was pretty cheery herself, but Maki was like turning the volume up to ear-splitting levels.

"Yeah! She was telling me about you. My name's Maki Shimizu! I'm glad we got to meet up here!"

"Y-yeah, me too, thanks," she said as Maki half forced her into a handshake. "But um, I'm sorry, but why are you calling me 'boss'?"

"Ahh, that's just a bad habit of Maki's."

"It's not a bad habit!" Maki half chortled before turning back toward Chiho, hand still locked with hers. "Lemme tell you, Yusa and Rika are *huge* to me. Like, *way* more than just having a nice friend at work 'n' stuff. They told me to stop calling 'em 'boss,' but that's sorta what you are to Yusa at work, right? So let's go with that!"

"Huh?! Um, geez, I—I really can't!"

What is this girl going on about? It's like talking to a space alien.

"See, I *told* you it's a bad habit. Calling people younger than you 'boss' is just weird."

"Aw, come on!" Maki protested, still smiling. "If you heaped *that* much praise upon her, then whether she's still in high school or not, she's gotta be someone incredible!"

"Well, maybe, but that doesn't mean you can call her whatever you want, Maki."

"What did you say to her, Yusa?" the slightly embarrassed Chiho asked.

"Oh, nothing out of the ordinary," Emi half apologized, "but Maki can get kinda impulsive sometimes, so…"

"Right, but I remember that Rika talks about her sometimes, too! Like, about this crazy awesome high schooler who's in one of her friend circles. That's you, right, boss?"

"Oh, I—I wouldn't say *crazy* awesome…"

"And if both Yusa and Rika have that to say about ya, then what kinda girl would I be if I didn't show you a little respect, huh?!"

"Yeah…"

The kind of girl, it seemed, who naturally put an exclamation point after nearly every thought she had.

"So anyway, is that okay if I call you that?"

"I—I really wish you wouldn't try to act all weirdly polite with someone younger than you, I mean…!"

"Okay, then as your elder, I'm reserving the right to call you 'boss,' then!"

"I'm sorry, Chiho. Maki's just been kinda wired these past two or three days."

Nothing seemed to discourage Maki. It was enough to annoy even Chiho.

"Well, what'd you expect?! Here you are, Emi Yusa, looking to *me* for help! What kind of woman wouldn't step up at a time like that?! I'm just keeping on my toes, is all!"

"She-she's just here to hang out a bit and chat," Yusa said. "If you keep that up, you're seriously gonna scare her, so could you turn it down a bit, Maki?"

"Okay!" She sat down, meekly obeying Emi's instructions. Once everyone else in the room was sufficiently chill, Emi started talking.

"Anyway, this is Maki Shimizu. She joined Rika and me at Dokodemo after we got hired. You're a…sophomore, right? At Waseta University?"

"W-Waseta?!"

Chiho's eyes shot open at the mention of one of Japan's most prestigious colleges.

"Oh, it's nothing *that* big. I just applied because that's what my parents told me to do. I really wanted to go to a music academy."

"Well, yeah, but it's not like Waseta just lets anyone in for a reason like that…"

The revelation honestly flustered Chiho. It was said you needed a college education to do pretty much anything these days, but that didn't mean all universities were the same. Some were known for being tough, for taking a real effort to get into. Waseta, nestled in the Tokyo neighborhood of Takadanobaba, was on the upper end of "tough." It took work to make it there, Chiho thought.

"True, but you know, I worked hard! I always work hard at school 'n' stuff. You know, I used to run track in high school, and that discipline kinda stuck with me. Ooh, I'm really trying to hold back right now, guys!"

"Oh…"

Being a college sophomore meant Maki was at least three years older than Chiho, but all this "boss" stuff and her general peppiness were really beginning to rub her the wrong way.

"Yeah," Emi mumbled, "she acted that way around Alas Ramus at first, too."

"Well, if you're bringing your relatives in to see me, Yusa, I gotta treat them the same way I treat you!"

So that's how she explained the child, Chiho thought. Maki didn't know who either of them truly were, and Rika probably didn't blab about it, either.

"Plus, she's cute!"

"Ah, don't take Relax-a-Bear, Maki-Sis!"

Said Relax-a-Bear plush must've belonged to Maki. It was roughly the same height as Alas Ramus, and she did *not* like the idea of Maki picking it up.

"See? So cute!"

"Y-yeah…"

She was cute, Chiho agreed. But there was something about the way that absolutely no rebuke worked against Maki. Something about it reminded her of Sariel, and the unique talent he had for driving Kisaki insane. But she thought, maybe that was part of the reason Emi was crashing at her place.

"So," Emi blurted out, watching her from the side, "you know, I came here because I wanted to talk to her about college, and admissions, and stuff."

"Oh?!" In a word, it shocked Chiho. "You're gonna go to a *Japanese* university?!"

Oops.

Chiho, immediately regretting her phrasing, shot a look toward Maki.

"Well," she calmly replied, "she might want to consider going overseas, too. Especially if she's graduated from a missionary school. It'd be a waste not to consider that!"

That seemed to explain Emi's backstory for Maki well enough. On the floor at MgRonald, she had pretended to be back in Japan from an extended period overseas—a tale she probably made up from the moment she applied to Dokodemo.

"Yeah, so among my friends, Maki's about the only one I can talk about college stuff with, so…"

Maki's eyes literally sparkled. "Ooh, what an honor!"

"So between that and the other stuff I've been dealing with, I've been chilling out here after work for the past little while, going out to eat and hanging out and stuff. Maki gave me a tour of her university today, too."

"They let nonstudents inside?"

"Oh, sure!"

Grade schools were quite a different story, but unless they were *really* small or *really* secretive, most universities in Japan allowed anyone to stroll around the premises, as well as access some of their academic facilities.

"It depends on the faculty, but you can even attend some classes on an audit basis without being admitted! Yusa didn't do that, but we did have lunch at the cafeteria!"

"Really?!"

This was a fresh surprise for Chiho. She knew from the placement program at her school that some private universities held welcome events for prospective students, but she had no idea campuses were so freewheeling with whom they let go inside. The idea of someone besides students and faculty milling around a high school was at best weird, at worst criminal.

"Yeah." Maki nodded wistfully. "I didn't know about that until the open-campus events I attended my last year in high school, too. But as long as you qualify, you can go to college no matter how old you are. They have cultural classes that are open to the general public, and you see businesspeople, researchers, and folks from other colleges on campus all the time. It's not like there are uniforms like in high school, and outside of, like, the research labs and libraries, you're free to go wherever you want, really. Probably a different story with some of the fancier private girls' schools, but…"

"Neat…"

"It was a lot of fun," Emi chimed in. "Like, everything seemed so new and fresh to me. And the cafeteria was really great for the price! Lots of different places to choose from."

"You can choose?"

"Well, there's the cafeteria run by the college," Maki explained, "but then there's the local food co-op, and there are a couple fancier places for the faculty, if you're willing to pay a bit more. You get a pretty wide selection!"

"Oh…"

There was, of course, only one cafeteria at Sasahata North High School, a place that—by and large—sold out of food before lunch break even ended. For Chiho, who had only a vague idea what "college life" was, most of what Maki described was beyond her imagination.

"I mean, the only thing I'd worry about is…" Maki brought a hand to her chin and gave an off-putting grin. "You know, Yusa, you're really beautiful, so I wonder if some of the seedier guys in your college would start targeting you. But hey, you'll have Alas Ramus running interference for you, huh?"

"You—you mean they'd hit on her?" Chiho asked, having only heard about this in the media so far in her life.

"Pretty much, yeah. I mean, you hear about how men don't really give a damn about romance these days, but you still get some pretty active dudes in college!"

"Wow…"

Another new thing for Chiho to learn, although she wasn't sure she agreed with Maki on that count.

"But you know, boss, I bet you'll have to deal with some tough things in college. At the start of the year, all the clubs open up to new members, and lemme tell you, at the events and stuff, all the clubs just descend on cute girls like you. They're like buzzards!"

She wasn't quite sure what Maki was talking about, but all this new information about what to expect in a couple years was starting to make Chiho's head swim.

"By the way, boss, you're in your second year of high school, right? So one more year before college? You're probably getting a lot of unsolicited advice about where to go, huh?"

"Uh..."

Chiho's head was no longer swimming.

It was the first time anyone had brought the topic up with her in a while. But it was true. High school lasted three years in Japan; she was now over halfway through her second, and at least a few of the students around her were starting to sweat their college admission exams.

"I mean, I'm not one to talk since it's not like I went to my first choice, and I probably sound like I'm just lecturing you from my high horse or whatever, but... You know, it's important that you have *some* kind of goal in mind, or else it'll be really hard to find motivation for college—like, before and after admission, I mean. So right now would be a great time for you to start thinking a little along those lines, like making a list of the kinds of things you wanna do. Nothing too fancy, but just to get the ball rolling."

"What I want to do, huh?"

Now Chiho was flustered for quite different reasons from when Maki first accosted her at the door. To her, the only thing that really mattered was her hope that she could keep her life with Maou, and Ashiya and Urushihara, and Emi and Suzuno and Alas Ramus, in peace. But ahead of that, she was also a high school student in Japan, and at this point in her life, she had things to do. And as long as she kept doing them, she'd be at her third and final year in high school in the blink of an eye.

"College..."

Year three would force her to start thinking about higher education, whether she wanted to or not. The question bothered her a little when she was hired at the MgRonald by Hatagaya station, but now her life was much, much different. She always knew, in a vague way, that college was a choice available to her. But it would take hard work and time. There were several people on the staff who planned to leave MgRonald because they were about to graduate from college and needed to hit the business-recruitment circuit—find a "real" job. Someday, before long, she'd have to devote a lot of her time to the college-admissions treadmill, too.

If Chiho just wanted to go to any college, her current grades would be zero hindrance to that. But—not that Maki mentioned it—just moving on to university, without really thinking about what she was doing, would undoubtedly lead to regrets later. She couldn't make her parents pay for four years in college that had no substance to it—and most of all, if she decided to take the easy way and make no effort of her own, she'd lose the right to be alongside Maou and Emi.

She thought through all of that in a single instant. It didn't result in any conclusion, however.

"College, huh? I feel like the more I think about it, the less I know. But are you gonna go to Waseta, Yusa?"

Emi smiled at the muddled question, but shook her head at it. "Oh, no way. I don't have the prerequisites, and I looked at some of Maki's college study guides, but I could barely even decipher the sample exams."

"The past exams? Um, could I take a look, maybe?"

"Go right ahead. I brought 'em in from my parents' place because Yusa said she was thinking about it. Um, which was it... Red spine, red spine..."

Maki slowly got up and took a book off the shelf—WASETA UNIVERSITY PAST EXAM QUESTIONS, the cover read. Chiho thumbed through it for a little while. Smoke shot out of her ears.

"This is...just..."

It wasn't totally incomprehensible. Just *generally* so. It was hard to decipher what was even being asked at times.

"Yeah, and I haven't studied in years, so there's no way I could pass an exam like that in one shot. And it's not like I'm fully committed to studying for this, either. It was just, like, I kinda wondered what being a college student was like, so..."

"Well, you speak all kinds of English, Yusa, so you got a head start! Do a little work, and I think it's totally possible!"

Maki stood back up, grabbed a compact notebook PC from the corner, and brought it back to the sofa. It was a super-slim model, far superior in every way to the ancient type Urushihara had, and when it booted up, Maki showed the screen to Emi.

"Also, Yusa, if you're looking for universities around Tokyo with a good agriculture program, here's a few of them."

"Agriculture... Oh!"

The keyword made Chiho's eyes burst open.

"Along those lines, the Tokyo University of Agriculture springs to mind first, but Meiji and its Ikuta campus have programs, too, and—you know, it's really hard to find a place that doesn't have one. Fusou, for example. And even then, there are all kinds of specialties you can pursue, like animal husbandry or life science or horticulture or urban planning. Kitazato University has a lot of neat faculties like that, along with a bunch of the public schools out in the country a little."

"Ooh, can I look at this for a bit?"

"Sure! All these names link to their webpages."

Emi began to tap at Maki's computer, her attitude 20 percent curious, 80 percent serious.

"What about you, boss? Anything you got your heart set on yet?"

"Me?"

The sudden question almost made Chiho drop the study guide in her hands.

"Well, um, not really, except I wanna go somewhere strong in English..."

That was what she wrote in the college-placement Q&A sheet they had her fill out back in spring. There wasn't much thought behind it, but she wasn't as set upon it as Emi apparently was with agriculture. English had even more subdivisions and specialties than farming, she knew—really, no matter what she majored in, English would be involved somehow.

"Oh, you thinking about studying abroad?"

"Abroad?! Ooh, I—I haven't thought that far! I haven't, but..."

But then why study English?

For now, all she could think of was how nice it'd be to chat more with the non-Japanese customers at MgRonald.

"Sounds like maybe you don't really know what you wanna do yet?"

"...Pretty much. I thought I had gotten over that before, but..."

"Mmm, makes sense." Maki nodded, shot a look at Emi to make sure she was still distracted by her college search, then sidled up to Chiho. "You know," she half whispered, "this is just some advice I got from other people..."

"Y-yeah?"

There wasn't much point to the act. There wasn't anyone else in the room, and Emi was stealing glances at them anyway, which made Chiho feel more than a little awkward.

"But if you don't know what to do now, I'd recommend going someplace where you have a lot of choice. That way, when you *do* find that something important to you, you'll be all set for it."

"Someplace with a lot of choice...?"

"Right. You don't strike me, boss, as the kinda gal who's counting on marrying some dude with a high-paying job and riding that out your whole life. So if you can't think of anything you want to do, then... You know, for now, just keep studying, and go for a nice, all-round kind of package until the application deadline."

"What do you mean?"

The first sentence of Maki's advice didn't seem to dovetail too well with the second in Chiho's mind.

"Well, like, yeah, Waseta's a really well-known, big-name university, but there's a lot of relatively no-name colleges that have, like, really great programs that let you do super high-level research. If you got something driving you, then by all means, don't just look at rankings or brand value; check out the research-driven places, too. You'll run into some great friends that way, too. Of course, if we're talkin' Tokyo or Kyoto University–level, that's a different story, but… You get me so far?"

"Yeah, I think I do. I'm definitely not thinking of *those* two."

Chiho was confident that she was a pretty good student, but in her mind, Tokyo University might as well be located beyond Ente Isla.

"All right. So if you aren't sure what to aim for, just try to score the best college you can, so when you *do* find that thing, you can switch right to that. It's kind of taking the long way compared to having a clear goal at the start, but it beats having nothing to aim for at all, don't you think?"

"Sure…"

She didn't know if this advice was based on Maki's own experience, but something about her motivational speaker–like approach struck her.

"I have this friend—she's graduated now—and she got a job offer for this really huge bank conglomerate, but she just said 'no' right out to it. I'm talking, like, the kind of bank where you can spit and hit one of their ATMs. It would've been a huge salary to start with out of college! You just know she would've made her whole extended family proud if she took it. She could've impressed all her friends, and she could've worked internationally, too. But she turned it down and joined another company she ran into while she was job hunting. And what kind of company do you think it was?"

Chiho made a suggestion. Maki immediately shook her head.

"She went to a company that makes *ship propellers*. She's busy polishing these huge propellers at a factory somewhere in Hiroshima. So, shipbuilding, basically."

Like I could've guessed that, Chiho thought. But she understood Maki's point.

"She told me her entire family screamed at her for turning down that mega-bank. The job placement center at college pleaded with her to reconsider! But she stood firm. She was all like, 'I want to support Japan's shipbuilding industry,' and off she went. She was texting me the other day to brag about how they shipped this propeller that's, like, three stories tall to some joint in Australia. And maybe people look at that and are like, 'Here's this girl who could've been set for life, but she settled for a ton less money to pursue her dreams.' But she loves ships, and she loves being in an environment where she's working with them every day. That's pretty hard to achieve, when you think about it, huh? And sure, she's not making huge sums of money, but it's not bad, either."

Maki didn't mean to say there were no dreams, no great mission to undertake, working for a large firm. She simply brought up an example of someone who worked hard to make as many choices available to herself as possible.

"So like, you have all these universities and trade schools and companies, and they all offer different kinds of choices to you. What you should do, boss, is find the place that lets you spread your choices out as much as possible, is what I say. I know I'm a whopping three years older than you, but that's what I can tell you from my experience."

"Oh, no, it's good stuff..."

"Of course, if you got a lead on something that'll, um, keep you set for life, that's easy street, pretty much. But that's a thing of the past these days."

"For life... Oh!"

Chiho took the hint. She meant the idea of getting married after graduation. The smoke shooting out of her ears turned to steam, her face turning red as if something just exploded inside her. Her imagination tended to run wild with subjects like these, and she never resented herself more for it.

It was too easy a reaction for Maki to read. She grinned and brought her face closer to her.

"Oooh, boss, do I detect...?"

"No, no, no, no! No! I'm not thinking anything!!"

"Wow! So you got a little Cupid plucking at your cute li'l heart-strings, huh?"

"Ahhhhhhhhhh..."

"Stop picking on Chiho, Maki!"

"Okaaay," Maki sighed, leaning back at Emi's admonishment. Chiho took that moment to gather her breath and take as much distance from Maki as the tiny room allowed her. *This girl's dangerous. She goes in for the kill even faster than Rika.*

"Well, enough joking—"

"How much of that was a joke?!" Chiho sternly protested.

Maki bowed her head, not looking too regretful about it. "Sorry, sorry. But you know, things have been really high-tension around here. I was just having a little fun!"

It didn't console Chiho much. Being toyed with like that would annoy anyone.

"But I'm kind of being serious, too! I mean, just thinking what you can do right now to keep from losing out later. I think that'll help you find a lot of direction, and stuff."

Maki gave a glance behind her.

"You know, Yusa told me something a little while ago—and ever since then, college has been a lot more fun for me."

"Wh-whoa, Maki?! What are you…?"

Emi's face reddened at becoming the center of conversation.

"Oh, I remember, girl! I know I'm a wimp with alcohol and people say I act all mean when I'm drunk, but I never black out! I still treasure that advice, y'know!"

"Stop!!" Emi, faced with this unexpected knockout blow, looked ready to faint. "I—I told you, it's not like I've done anything myself yet! That was just a bunch of haughty BS I told you! Just forget about it!"

"Nuh-uh! I mean, it literally changed the trajectory of my student life. You never know when you'll run into a turning point like that, huh?"

"Quit being so stupid! Ugh…!"

It seemed to Chiho she wasn't the only one Maki was leading around by the ear.

"Maki-Sis, Maki-Sis!"

"Hmm? What's up, Alas Ramus?!"

The child toddled up to her, dragging the Relax-a-Bear behind her.

"Daddy!"

"Daddy?"

"Mmm."

"Whoa, what do you mean, Alas Ramus?"

"Alas Ramus?!"

Emi and Chiho both expressed intense alarm at the innocent girl's behavior. But the bombshell was unleashed without a moment's thought for them:

"Daddy. Mommy 'n' Chi-Sis like Daddy a lot!"

"……Alas Ramus?"

"Oo?"

"If you tell me about 'Daddy,' I'll give you that Relax-a-Bear."

"Maki!!"

"Ms. Shimizu!!"

They both stepped up to stop the malevolent Maki from snaring this tender waif with bribery. But there was no taking back what was said. Alas Ramus immediately understood the offer. Her eyes shone as her small lips parted.

"Daddy, um, Daddy is Maou!"

"Maou? That's his name?"

"Ms. Shimizu, please stop! You should be ashamed of yourself, bribing little children like that!"

"You're making me angry, Maki!"

All three ventured on, paying no mind to the neighbors downstairs. But Alas Ramus's one-girl play continued anon.

"Maou… Name. Mmm, yeh, Daddy, Maou."

"Maou, huh! Well, that's a funny name!"

They couldn't physically close the child's mouth, so Emi and Chiho attempted to close Maki's instead.

"Daddy, um… He loves money. But he's poor. And, uhhh… foo-gal?"

"Um, Alas Ramus, I think that's enough…"

Chiho didn't want Maki to know about Maou, of course, and having this sweet little child refer to her own father as "poor" almost made her cry on the spot. But just before she could put a finger to her lips and shush her:

"And, and, Daddy is reawwy…lonewy."

"Oh?"

"…Alas Ramus?" asked Emi, frozen to the spot even as she had Maki in a wrestling-style headlock.

"Maou's lonely?" Chiho exclaimed.

"Daddy reawwy likes his friends. He wants 'em to…stay. Not go."

"Y-Y-Yusa, I—I can't breathe…"

"Daddy likes his money, and, and he likes his fwiends, and he likes work. And dat's why Mommy 'n' Chi-Sis 'n' Suzu-Sis like Daddy!"

"I—I never said that…"

She knew it was pointless to deny it in front of her, but something about her "daughter" claiming that Emi loved Daddy was highly disturbing.

"And, and Daddy likes his friends, so…that's why he was mean to Mommy."

"…Alas Ramus? Do you mean…?"

Chiho took her arms off Maki and turned toward the child. She had the feeling Alas Ramus was trying to discuss something very important. Emi must have picked up on it as well, because she removed her arms from her groaning friend Maki and turned to the toddler.

"Alas Ramus," Emi asked, "when you said 'Mommy'…are you talking about Laila?"

She nodded.

"Daddy likes work, he likes fwiends…but Mommy tried to make 'im work. For her. …Reawwy mean!"

Laila had tried to make Maou work for her. Emi and Chiho couldn't say what that meant—but somehow, it made a lot of sense to them. Everyone in their circle figured that Laila was trying to take a thorny situation, one involving all of Ente Isla, and place it in their laps. But both Emi and Maou had turned her down. They hadn't even listened to her. Why couldn't they inspire themselves to do even that? Something told them the answer lay somewhere within Alas Ramus's words.

"Tried to make him work, huh…?"

Alas Ramus, taken out of the hospital with Emi, wasn't there to hear the full story. There was no way she had a full grasp of Laila's intentions. But seeing Laila closer to her than ever before, and neither Maou nor Emi deigning to interact with her, must have seemed strange to the child's mind. She must have been looking for an answer.

"Alas Ramus?"

"Hi, Mommy!"

"That Relax-a-Bear belongs to Maki. I'll buy a new one for you when we get home, all right?"

"Reawwy?!" Her face shone, the meekness of a moment ago quite gone.

"Really. We have to go home for now, but I think the store will still be open in Shinjuku when we stop by."

Emi looked at the clock in the room. It was just before seven.

"Huhh? You're going home today, Yusa?!" said Maki, fully recovered from Emi and Chiho's tag-team attack but now shocked for a different reason.

"I've already stayed here two nights without any warning. I can't put any more trouble on you."

"Oh, you can stay here as many days as you want, Yusa!"

She sounded sincere enough, but Emi couldn't let that happen. "Sorry, but I'm good, honestly. I have someone staying at my place right now anyway."

"You mean that Maou person *bephpphhhhh* ftorry, sorry, sorry!"

It wasn't anything Maki thought too deeply about before saying it, but it was still enough to make Emi grab both of her cheeks at once, smiling the whole way.

"Listen, girl. Remember that friend from when I was overseas? I told you about that first thing."

"Mmph, yeph, yeph, ftorry… *Pahh*… But seriously, if you ever need anything, just give me a call. I'll be glad to help if I can!"

"Sure," she said, the smile returning to her face as she released her and gave her a loose kind of shoulder hug.

"Agh!"

"You were a big help."

"Oh, no, no, yerrelcome!" Maki said, putting her head over Emi's shoulder and nodding awkwardly a few times. And watching them, Chiho thought she knew why Emi had come to Maki.

"Come back soon! I mean it! Soon!"

After they walked out the door, Maki reluctantly seeing them off like they'd never meet again in this lifetime, Emi and Chiho boarded the Fukutoshin Line off Zoshigaya Station. They were headed back home to Eifukucho, and fortunately, their local train bound for Shinjuku-sanchome wasn't at rush-hour levels of crowd.

"I'm sorry, Chiho," Emi said once they found a pair of adjacent seats. "I guess I have this habit of getting you involved in my personal affairs."

Chiho took a moment to look at her reflection in the subway window, staring off into the distance. "Well," she said, "at least I think I know why you were at Ms. Shimizu's place now, Yusa."

"Rika suggested it. She thought my mind could use a reset somewhere. Like, with someone who isn't involved with Ente Isla or angels or Heroes or whatever."

This was Maki, after all, a woman who positively adored Emi. Even on a normal day, she went full-court press on her; if Emi was in some kind of trouble, she'd no doubt do everything she could to make her feel better. Maki didn't seem to know the truth about her, so it wasn't like Emi could've told her anything *too* deep—but that college campus visit wasn't strictly for funsies, either. Emi was at least somewhat serious about discussing higher education with her former coworker, Chiho felt, and Maki must've seized on that and wanted to help her out. Right now, that was just the companion Emi needed, probably.

Emi ran a hand through the hair of Alas Ramus, who was currently wavering back and forth in her lap as she nodded off.

"You know, after I got off work at the Mag, I'd go meet up with Maki and we'd go out to eat, or hit the gym, or whatever. She wasn't surprised to see Alas Ramus at all, either. We went shopping for pajamas for her and everything. It's really helped me refresh, for the first time in a while... I'll have to compensate Eme for that later."

"I'm sure she'll understand."

"Probably, but I still need to make up for it. She'll have some food-related request for me, I bet. It's already giving me a headache."

"Hee-hee!"

Emi smiled at the laughter.

"...You know, I think I probably went too far back there, too. I've really come to look at it that way, the past few days."

"Oh?"

"It depends on how you look at it, but... I mean, I just spent the past couple days *using* Maki, essentially, to make myself feel better. Taking advantage of the fact she has no idea what's up with me. Doesn't it look that way to you?"

"That's what friends are, though, aren't they?" Chiho gave a light shake of her head. "It's not like Ms. Shimizu was looking to get anything back for it, and I'm sure you'll kind of unconsciously make up for it later on with her, right?"

"Yeah, but... Oh, how to put it? Sure, Laila's put me through a bunch of crap, but I can't deny that she's expended a lot of effort for my sake, too. In her own way. Not because she needs me for her goals, but just because I'm her daughter, I think. I don't know. I'm sorry. I'm not making any sense."

"No, it's fine," she replied with a nod. "I understand. I doubt Nord would marry someone who saw you as nothing but Emilia the holy sword–wielding Hero. I'm not in full support of her or anything... but you and she have been separated so long, I honestly think she didn't know what to do with herself. That's why it all fell apart like that."

"Yeah. So I think that...you know, I'm ready to meet her halfway a little. But if you want me to call her 'mom,' I'm not the least bit interested in that."

"Sure. And that's fine. That's a lot to ask out of nowhere. And she might be your biological mom, but to you, she's just this stranger who stepped in from the crowd, you know? Nobody you *know*. It's not like you'll immediately learn everything about each other on the first day. I've lived with my parents for seventeen years, and we still argue about stuff sometimes."

"I have trouble picturing you arguing with your parents, Chiho. Like, ever."

"Oh, I'm not that good a girl."

"If you aren't, that makes everybody else in the universe down-right evil."

They shared a laugh over this. Then Emi recalled a term Chiho used:

"Nobody I know, huh...?"

She had heard it before, a long time ago, from someone else—before she knew where Alas Ramus really came from.

"Who was it?"

"Nobody you know."

That was the brazen way that man described the angel who once saved his life.

Certainly, at the time, Emi didn't think much of anything about Laila. She was her mom, she was out there somewhere, and that was it. She didn't really *know* her, and when Emeralda and Albert brought her up in conversation, it didn't really move her heart and soul the way news of her father's survival did.

But she still knew Laila was her mother. Maybe that was why Maou kept his mouth shut. About the fact that her own mother saved the life of mankind's worst enemy.

"..."

"Mm..."

She clutched at Alas Ramus a little tighter than before, bringing her body closer.

"Yusa?"

What benefit would it bring Maou *not* to talk about Laila back then? She couldn't think of any. Having secret intel about Laila's past didn't give him any advantage over Emi—if that was his aim, he would've been far better off hiding the origins of the Yesod and Alas Ramus instead.

If he could have had any motivation…

"…Oh, give me a break."

…it'd be to avoid hurting her feelings. To keep her from worrying herself sick.

This all happened just after Sariel came to Japan, when Emi had begun having doubts about the angels and their intentions. If she knew that Laila had rescued the Devil King himself, it could've been devastating. She was still being driven by her pride as a Hero and her duty to slay that Devil King. If he let on the truth to her, it'd create too much of a conflict between her Heroic mission and what her mother did. It'd destroy her. She wouldn't be able to do what was best for Alas Ramus.

"And he calls himself…Devil King…"

It irritated her to know that Maou could see all of that. And she wasn't confident enough to avow that learning the truth wouldn't have ruined her.

"Mommy?"

The drowsy Alas Ramus listlessly looked up at Emi, noticing the extra force she was held up with. Emi responded by burying her face in the little child's shoulder, as if escaping from the gaze. She wanted some other reason, some motivation for Maou to hide the truth about Laila from her. He must've been trying to get a leg up, somehow—or hiding it gave him some kind of edge. That had to be it. Otherwise, it just made no sense. It didn't…

"You okay, Yusa?"

"……Yeah. I'm fine," Emi said, looking back up.

The train arrived at Higashi-Shinjuku Station in another few moments, one stop before their line change. The PA system announced that they would be stopped on the platform for approximately three minutes to allow an express train to pass by.

"Yusa…"

"I know." She let out a heavy sigh and looked upward.

"Did you stop breathing just now?"

"Huh?"

The sight of Emi's uplifted face gave Chiho concern.

"I just mean…"

"Hmm?"

"Your face is all red."

"…Huh?"

She brought a hand to her face—not like she could tell her skin color by touch. But if the pale bluish-white of the subway's interior lights made her look that way, she had to be blushing a little bit, at least. Why? She knew. No point denying it now.

"Chiho, I…"

"Yes?"

"…I'm not sure I mind all this much."

The words came out freely. She didn't have to summon any courage for it.

The departure bell rang. The doors closed, and the train set off once more.

"Huh? Don't mind what?" asked Chiho, raising an eyebrow. The sudden crackling of the automatic PA system prevented her from receiving an answer.

"Emergency stop! All passengers, brace yourselves! Emergency stop!"

Before anyone had a chance to brace themselves, the freshly departed train slammed on the brakes. It made even the seated Emi and Chiho lose their balance, forcing Emi to hold on tight to her child.

"Wh-whoa!"

"Agh!"

With the sound of screeching wheels, the train quickly bled off whatever acceleration the past few seconds allowed it. It was no longer rush hour, but given the subway line's location—connecting the two mega-stations of Ikebukuro and Shinjuku—a decent number of passengers were very suddenly subjected to the law of momentum. Some fell to the floor.

"Chiho, you all right?!"

"I-I'm fine. How's Alas Ramus...?"

"Ooo, scary!"

By the time it stopped, Alas Ramus was looking around the car, wide-eyed but otherwise unfazed. Nobody else nearby seemed too banged up, and the atmosphere was already turning back to normal.

A somewhat harried-sounding conductor chose that moment to get on the PA.

"Ahh, this train has just engaged its emergency-brake system... The train made an emergency stop after a public emergency button was pressed up ahead at Shinjuku-sanchome Station. Umm..."

With every extended pause, they could hear the sound of machines operating and the radio springing to life in the conductor's room.

"We apologize for the inconvenience to our passengers, but this train will be stopped here for a period of time..."

"Pretty strong brakes, huh?"

"Hopefully, it's not some huge accident," Chiho replied as they settled back down. The rest of the passengers were similarly calm, if a little annoyed at the delay. Some were reading; some were listening to music; some were tapping away at their phones. One of them was already back to snoring in his seat—a veteran train commuter, no doubt.

As Emi took a few moments to scope them all out, amid the oddly quiet atmosphere of a stopped train, the speaker returned to life.

"Umm, this is an announcement from the conductor's room. We have received word that a passenger has fallen onto the track at Shinjuku-sanchome Station. This was why the emergency-stop button was pressed, which brought this train to a halt earlier. We will begin traveling again once our team is sure that the track is safe for navigation. Once again, we apologize for any inconvenience placed upon our passengers and their schedules. Thank you."

"Guess you can't blame the train company for that," Emi remarked as she stared at the ceiling. Then she looked down at Chiho, who had an oddly baffled look on her face.

"Hmm? What's up?"

"Oh, um... I don't know, I just had a weird thought," she replied, her voice unusually soft.

"A weird thought?"

"Did you see that thing going around the Net a couple days ago? About the jargon used in news broadcasts and what it really means?"

"What's that?" Emi asked.

"Well, you know how we call the bathroom 'Number Ten' over at the Hatagaya MgRonald, right? So customers can't tell what we're talking about. Kind of like that. You hear terms on the news like *seriously injured* or *serious condition* or *he was struck by the vehicle* all the time, and they're used to kind of whitewash over all the gory stuff that *really* happened."

"Ohhh, I heard about that, I think. Like, how the conductor might say 'a passenger has entered the track' when there's really been a sexual assault or something. You think it's that kind of thing?"

As serious as that would be, Emi didn't see why that required slamming on the brakes.

"No. I thought so at first, but the conductor said someone 'fell' on the track."

"Oh? I wasn't really paying attention."

"Can you do that, though? At Shinjuku-sanchome?"

"Huh?"

"'Cause I'm pretty sure there are automatic doors on the platform to prevent that, at least on the Fukutoshin subway line. It'd take a lot of effort to 'fall' on the track."

"Geez, Chiho, you're starting to spook me. I'm sure it's just a figure of speech. Maybe someone caught their foot in the gap between the train and the platform, huh? You hear about that a lot."

"Yeah, true."

Chiho wasn't entirely sure why she'd brought it up herself. But something still seemed off to her. Looking at her phone, it was now past seven. Shinjuku-sanchome Station would be pretty full of passengers—and someone *fell* on the track? Not 'entered' or some other euphemism?

She knew she was worrying excessively. She knew her time with

Maou and Emi had made her mentally prepare for the most preposterous of situations at times. *It'd be nice if the train could start up again. Emi was just about to get over her issues. Let's get her to the station and keep anything else from happening.*

But Chiho's plaintive prayer was, perhaps, too far underground to reach heaven. Out of nowhere, the interior lights went out.

"Wha—?!"

With nothing but the small fluorescent lights lining the tunnel to illuminate the car, it was almost pitch-black, save for the rapidly flickering phone screens. Some people were already hurriedly turning on their flashlight function.

Chiho's eerie imaginative skills unnerved Emi, but now that something really was going on, she used her left hand to bring her friend close as she scanned the area. All the phone flashlights made the car remarkably visible end-to-end, showing just how shaken everyone was. One woman was already sobbing.

"Um, this is the conductor's room," came the somewhat excited voice through the speaker, the radio chatter playing loudly behind it indicating that this was not part of the routine. *"Ahh, the interior illumination on all cars of this train is currently, um, offline. The emergency lighting will turn on shortly. We ask that all passengers please remain calm and wait for instructions from crewmembers before... Huh?"*

It was a noble effort, saying what needed to be said despite the intensity of it all, but the voice cut off midsentence.

"Wh-what's...? Someone on the tracks..."

"What...?"

Emi's face tensed at the voice. The conductor was clearly no longer following the spiel in the training guides.

"Somebody push the emergency talk button!" a passenger half shouted at this nerve-racking performance. Emi looked around for it. It was too far to reach without letting go of Chiho. She hesitated.

"A1875T calling in! S-someone's on the tracks! Coming from Shinjuku-sanchome Station... Oh!"

The conductor, finally realizing he had left the PA system on, flipped the switch on it. The timing he chose provided nothing but uneasy suspense for his passengers. They could all tell that something far from the norm was happening—and nobody was telling them what. The eerie quietness, coupled with the latent anxiety, only served to quicken the spread of fear.

Emi stayed on her guard, nervously swallowing. Alas Ramus was in her right arm, Chiho in her left, and she was half off the edge of her seat, ready to take action at any time as she strained through the shouting for any unusual sounds when—

"Mommy!!"

The warning came from Alas Ramus.

The train, all ten cars of it, began moving in the opposite direction from where it should have been going. Screams erupted in the car.

"Yusa!"

"Stay still! Don't go away from me! Ngh!"

Then, a sharp impact. This was no longer just a car idly rolling down a hill. It felt like all ten cars were colliding against one another as the entire train edged backward.

"What—what's going on?! …Again?!"

There was no sign that the conductor would offer further guidance. The train lurched, then lurched again. Then another time.

"Y-Yusa, could this be…?"

"Yeah," Emi nodded. "I don't want to think so, but…"

She could tell through the windows that the tunnel was still being illuminated by small fluorescent lights at regular intervals. There was no sound to warn the passengers of any incoming impact—the tunnel itself wasn't collapsing. And that voice, just before it was cut off: "Someone on the tracks." Someone who, now, may very well have been attacking the train.

"Yusa, I…"

Chiho looked at Emi, ready to act. But Emi shook her head, cutting her off.

"No. I can't leave you in here, Chiho."

She wanted to leave the train at once, to gauge what clearly was an emergency now, but she couldn't leave Chiho inside a train car she couldn't guarantee was safe at all. Bringing her out of the car, on the other hand, would be plunging her into a situation potentially just as dangerous. She couldn't help but look at the sign above her: IN CASE OF EMERGENCY, DO NOT EXIT THE TRAIN UNLESS INSTRUCTED SO BY A CREWMEMBER.

"But if we don't do something... Mmph!"

The train lurched once more as they wallowed in indecision.

"All right. Let's do this, Chiho."

"O-okay."

"When was the last time you had a 5-Holy Energy β?"

Chiho's eyes shot open. "...!"

"I need to do something pretty large scale here. You get affected by holy energy easily, so I don't want you fainting from it again. Just try to summon up as much force as you've got for me, okay? Can you do that?"

"I'll be okay." She nodded. "I had one pretty recently. I used an Idea Link on the day I went to Urushihara's hospital room, so I filled up then..."

"Yeah, I heard from Eme. That was pretty creative. Let's talk about it later."

Emi smiled a bit, then looked upward, bracing herself for anything as she gauged the train's direction of travel. Chiho, just as instructed, began to take deep breaths, attempting to calm her alarm bell–like heartbeat. She could feel a warm sort of strength pulse through her body, and then, when it reached just the right level, she felt it being subsumed by an even greater force. It took her aback a little, but her feelings, and her instincts, told her this was Emi's holy force.

"...Everyone else should be all right now," Emi nervously whispered, even as she concentrated. There would be no wavering now. "Chiho, Alas Ramus, cover up your ears!"

"Okay."

"Okeh!"

Without questioning it, Chiho and Alas Ramus obeyed the order. Then:

"Ah!"

Chiho yelped at the sharp, heavy impact that raced across her body. It was like a large wave coursed through the air, smashing against her.

"Wh-what was that?!"

"Get—get me out of here! When can we move?!"

The passengers were picking up on the anomaly, but nobody seemed to be affected as much as Chiho. It was treated as just another facet of the emergency surrounding them, adding more fuel to the flames.

"!!"

Emi, alone, stayed frozen, eyes transfixed in the direction the train was going.

"Huh?!"

Suddenly, her eyebrows swung downward.

"A…a child?"

"Wh-what is it?"

"There's a child shaking the train."

"Huh? How do you…?"

"I sent off a short-range sonar bolt," Emi briskly replied. She stood up, taking her arm off Chiho. "It should be safe in here, but… This is bad. It's not normal."

Alas Ramus in hand, Emi lunged to her side and flew right out into the tunnel, in front of Chiho and the rest of the crowd. The next moment, she was outside, one hand on the car she had just left.

"Ah, Yusa…?"

"S-someone just went out the window!"

"Stay in here for now," Emi said as she sealed off all entrances and exits with her holy force. "It's too dangerous." The panicked passengers inside weren't knocking one another over, at least, which was a relief. The Yamanote Line, which ran in parallel with this subway line between Ikebukuro and Shinjuku, kept things from being wall-to-wall crowded here.

"All right. You felt that sonar bolt just now, right?! Who are you?!"

She glared at the shadow up ahead, one car's length away. She hadn't noticed when she boarded, but Emi was on the fifth of ten train cars. To her front and rear, she could hear the creaking of steel from the silvery boxes in the darkness.

"Thanks to you, the Fukutoshin Line's probably gonna stop running 'til tomorrow. That's gonna have a huge impact on a lot of the private lines around the city. I don't see any demonic force around here, but if you pull this crap in the middle of rush hour, don't be shocked if you resurrect the Devil King himself."

She couldn't help but bring up the possibility. She had done it herself, after all, after she and Suzuno stirred up a little ruckus in Shinjuku...or really, wrecked the whole place. But they were in a subway tunnel now, with only the dimmest of lighting. She knew from her sonar that the barely discernible figure before her was about the height of a human child. The problem was, she couldn't think of anyone who could pull off such violence around her right now.

The demons were tamed, thanks to the events in Heavensky. Apart from Sariel and Gabriel, both well used to life in Japan by now, the angels had cut off all ties to Earth. And it was hard to picture any of the human power brokers and would-be foes of Emi on Ente Isla sending an assassin her way. Emeralda and Albert would've handled all of them after the battle at Heavensky, and besides, Shiba and Amane would've immediately noticed such a traveler visiting from another world.

They glared at each other for a few seconds. It was broken only when a gust of wind blew from behind Emi toward the figure, imbued with the traditional odors of a subway tunnel.

""!!""

The figure's face shot upward, as if forced. As it did, Alas Ramus squirmed her way away from Emi's arm.

"Alas Ramus?"

"...Who's that?"

"Huh?"

"It looks the same...but...no. But the same. Who's that?"

"!!"

There was no time to put an end to the child's bizarre behavior.

With astonishing speed, the shadow closed the distance between them in a single bound.

"Ah...!! Alas Ramus!"

Almost reflexively, Emi transformed Alas Ramus into her holy sword, preparing for the mysterious figure's attack. Before she could:

"Wh-what on—?!"

Something that looked like the figure's arm stopped her blade, making her shout out in surprise.

She thought, at first, that she couldn't fully make out the childlike figure because of its dark robe, or maybe it was a coat of some sort? But that was a mistake. The shadow whose "arm" was crossing Emi's sword was just that—a shadow. A human silhouette, all but peeled from the ground, its eyes an ominous shade of crimson.

"Nhh!!"

Its strength was equally surprising. Emi couldn't tell how it was making the train cars shake like that, but its sudden charge was enough to make her stumble with her sword, jolting her back. This was no ordinary foe.

"What—what *are* you?!"

It was all beyond belief, but what made it worse was the sound of the impact. Metal against metal. It was a shade, a shimmering sort of dark flame bouncing in the air, but when her sword crossed it, a sharp clang pulsed along the tunnel, like a hammer striking an anvil. The vibration that raced across the blade to her palm told her that the Better Half had just hit metal.

"Mommy! It's real strong!"

"I know!"

Alas Ramus seemed just as alarmed, her tone sterner than usual as she warned her mother.

"Ugh, it's too *early* for me to go back to reality! Why can't you let me enjoy something *besides* the norm for a change?!"

Nobody was there to point out that Emi's definition of *the norm* was the opposite of most people's. To her, the couple of days spent with Maki was *away* from the norm. Being attacked by a mysterious black shadow inside a subway tunnel, as much as she hated to admit it, wasn't. Not even she was optimistic enough to assume this was a random attack on a train she just happened to be riding.

"One good thing about this, though…" She grinned fearlessly, focusing upon her blade. "It's so dark inside and out, as long as I don't generate too much weird light, I can fight *exactly* the way I want."

Whenever she made up her mind to fight, Emi would usually transform, her hair and eyes changing to reflect her angelic self. But in this tunnel, that was too much dazzling illumination to risk. So she focused just on powering up her sword instead.

"*Ooooooooo!*"

This seemed to surprise Alas Ramus, making her coo in the most darling—yet excited—fashion. It almost made Emi laugh, but she couldn't put too much burden on the child. She couldn't let this shadowmancer overpower her, of course, but if that was all she cared about, it'd be much simpler for her to transform and whip the snot out of it.

No, her sights were set on something else.

"Okay, um… Can we *please* get this over with before the maintenance guys make it here? Oof!"

Now it was Emi's turn to strike. It was a simple stroke, she aimed a massive swing at the crown of the shade's head.

It blocked the attack with nothing more than its crossed arms, generating sparks and an ear-splitting *clang*. The impact sent Emi reeling—but that was her plan.

She performed a somersault, as if leaping back from the strike, then unleashed a horizontal slash at the figure's unprotected torso.

"Yah!"

It moved to block it once more. But at that moment, she launched a full force heel kick upon the "face" of the dark figure, aimed right at the eyes. It tried to cover its head, but as it did, Emi aimed a piercing stab at its torso once more, with all her might.

"!"

"…!"

The edge of the holy sword, infused with as much force as it could take without transforming her, failed to penetrate even a millimeter. Emi winced as the impact traveled up her right hand. But it still fazed the shadowmancer, the blunt force applied to the middle of its frame making it stagger backward.

"Haaahhhh!!"

Emi seized the chance. Like a whirlwind, she sent her whole body spinning, smashing her sword against her foe. Each strike felt like she was simply banging against cold steel, but her foe still reared back, closing both arms to protect its face.

"You can't escape me! At least show yourself!!"

Emi's left leg kicked against the stagnant wall of air before her, sending a cannon-like roar echoing. She pressed on, her body hurtling like a cannonball toward the figure.

"My power shall exact judgment upon all those who disturb this world!!"

With this very non-Heroic shout, Emi filled the tunnel with the light of holy magic—for just an instant. For the length of a camera flash, short enough that it could be easily missed if one's eyes were elsewhere, she transformed. But in that instant, the holy sword made absolute contact with the enemy.

"?!"

It shuddered. There was no clanging now—but the blade didn't bite into the shadowmancer, either. It found no resistance at all, going straight through its body.

"*Huh?*"

Alas Ramus was just as flummoxed by the lack of substance as Emi was. Already back to normal form, the Hero twirled through the air, expecting the shade to counter her. But:

"Did...that work?"

She raised a quizzical eyebrow at the discrepancy between what she felt and what had unfolded before her. The shadowmancer's left arm was now...a human arm. As if it was wearing a marvelous, shape-shifting suit of armor until now, the figure shed its darkness all over the tunnel, revealing what was obviously a plain old arm.

It didn't *feel* like Emi had broken its armor at all. The shadow-mancer's arms felt like a single forged piece of metal, offering no give whatsoever—but now that she broke through it, it offered no more resistance than a piece of burlap. What could it mean? It meant Emi had the advantage, yes, but the arm her all-out strike had revealed had no wound upon it. How strange.

Now would normally be the time to continue with the attack, now that she found an effective approach. But the sheer uncanniness of it all made Emi hesitate. The shadow stared at the arm with its crimson eyes, never expecting this to happen.

"*It's through...the inside.*"

"What?"

"*It went through the inside just now.*"

Alas Ramus had rarely spoken as clearly in Emi's mind as she did now.

"*Mommy, the sword went through the inside. So much power went through the body, and it cut something else.*"

"Something else?"

"*Mommy, I know him. Don't hurt him anymore!*"

"Huh? But..."

"*We can break the shadow down, but he's still stronger. But if we cut the inside, I know he'll die. Please!*"

"But I can't just...!"

Alas Ramus suddenly seemed years older, eloquently expressing herself to her confused partner. And she wanted that young woman to put the sword down.

"What am I supposed to do, then?!"

But Emi's opponent didn't care. It wasn't even listening.

"Khh!"

The shadowmancer, back on its feet and left arm still fully visible, lunged back.

"*Mommy! Please! Stop!*"

"I—I can't!"

She didn't want to swing the Better Half against Alas Ramus's wishes. But the figure was playing for keeps. It bore enough power to exact serious damage upon Emi, and as long as she couldn't deploy the overly conspicuous Cloth of the Dispeller, she was forced to block it with her blade.

"I—I can't let this go on forever..."

But there *was* something different. The shadowmancer wasn't attacking with its human left arm. Perhaps it was the shadow armor that gave it strength, or at least the protection to go blow-to-blow with her. But she couldn't just slash at it. Alas Ramus pleaded with her not to, at all costs. The lack of any shadow didn't seem to make it any weaker, either—apart from not using its left arm, the shade attacked just as ferociously as before.

Just when Emi was starting to worry about how this battle would unfold...

"?!"

She saw a powerful light approach from the direction of Higashi-Shinjuku Station, the one the train had just left. Her blood froze.

Another train?

But the light was bobbing up and down, violently.

"Yusa!"

"Emilia!!"

The voices of Amane Ohguro and—very unexpectedly—Emeralda Etuva echoed across the tunnel.

"Emilia!"

"—!!"

Those two, and one more voice—the voice of someone who Emi figured might show up, but whom she absolutely did *not* want around her. She gritted her teeth.

Taking zero notice of Emi's effort to keep things dark, Laila came closer and closer to her, emanating a light stronger than either of the others.

"I can *not* believe you!!" Emi shouted. "What are you *doing*?! Are you trying to mess this whole thing up for me?!"

"Now's no time for that! Get away from that child! You can't fight him with the Yesod fragment you bear! Hurry!"

"What?!"

Don't give me that crap, Emi just barely had the time to think.

"Mommy!!"

But in those scant few moments when Laila distracted her, with Emeralda and Amane in tow—so quickly a regular person could've barely followed it, no matter how closely they looked—the shadow's exposed left arm extended itself close to Emi's body.

"Uh…!"

And then, in what would have been a mere few hundredths of an instant, many things happened. Laila came between Emi and the shade. Her shoulder brushed against the figure's arm.

"Aaahhhhh!!"

Her scream echoed across the tunnel. A lukewarm liquid splashed across Emi's face.

"…!"

Before she could determine what it was—

"Oh, crap! What is that freak doing?!"

"Laila! Emilia!!"

Amane joined the fray, stepping up to protect Emi and Laila from the shadowmancer, as Emeralda pushed Emi and the off-balance Laila to the side.

"E-Eme… What did you…?"

"Worry about it later!!"

"W-wait, Chiho's still…"

"Amane can take care of that! We need to get you and Alas Ramus as far away from that shadow as we can!"

"Wait… Wait, Chiho's… Laila, you're kidding me, what's going on here?"

Staring blankly at Amane, the shadow, and the train as they all shrank farther and farther away from her, Emi brought a hand to her face.

"Uh… Whoa, you were *thaaat* close to the next station?!"

Emeralda, Emi in her arm, expressed honest surprise as she flew toward the lights of Shinjuku-sanchome Station looming ahead. But Emi couldn't hear her. She turned to her side—only to find the bloodstained and pallid face of Laila, carried next to her. Her beautiful shoulder had been thoroughly smashed and bloodied—and Emeralda may not have known how angel bodies worked, but she knew that *this* angel needed treatment, fast. If anything happened to her, it'd cast yet another pall upon Emilia's heart.

"What... What's happening here? Did you put me up to this again?! What is your problem?! Huh?! How long are you gonna be a thorn in my side until you give up?! Why do you have to cause my friends so much trouble?!"

"Emilia!!"

Emeralda, seeing Emi lose control of herself, admonished her as loudly as she could. Emi didn't even hear that.

"*Answer* me!!"

"Emilia! Please, this can wait for later! Just keep quiet! I'm gonna have to fly under the platform doors so people don't see us!"

"Come on! Answer me!"

"Emilia, please...!"

In one arm, the unconscious Laila. In the other, Emi mercilessly barraging her. Emeralda wasn't sure she could keep on flying.

"Will you guys knock it off?"

It was a low, restrained voice, but it came through loud and clear to Emi and Emeralda, slashing through the heavy tunnel air.

"Bggph!!"

At that moment, Emeralda collided with something in the air—something soft, like silk. She pitched forward.

"Ah..."

The unexpected shift in momentum sent Emi and Laila away from her grasp. She watched them go, dumbfounded—but they never quite reached the hard steel tracks that lined the Shinjuku-sanchome platform.

"…Huhhh…?"

It took a moment for Emeralda to figure out what this thing was, this thing that—like water, or cotton, or a cloud—softened their momentum. It must have awed her a bit, as she blithely, drowsily stared at a figure above her, sitting atop a platform gate.

"Glad to see you guys are having a hell of a night."

"Uhh…"

He swung his legs up and down, irritatedly banging the leather heels of his shoes against the door.

"You know what time it is, Emeralda Etuva? It's seven thirty."

"Y-yesss?"

"I know you ain't used to life in Japan yet, so let me clue you in. Seven thirty's about the time people around here start thinking about dinner. It's the peak of the dinner rush. You understand me so far?"

"Y-yesss…?"

He was angry. Emeralda could tell that much. But the nature of his rage was so alien to her that she wasn't exactly sure how to deal with it.

"When it's the peak of the dinner rush, you know what that means? It means we get a ton of customers. A ton of customers means that the whole place gets *extremely* busy for the staff. You hear me?"

"Y-yesss, I dooo…"

"But ooh, golly, I guess I'm here, huh? Do you know what that means?"

"Umm…ummmmm…"

She didn't know, but it was bad. Whatever it was, this was galling him more than almost anything else could in his life.

"Look, what is *with* you bastards?! You all just constantly nag, nag, nag at me from your high horse, and you can't even keep *Chi* safe for half a second! Huh?!"

She shivered, stooping over to make herself smaller.

It was with a look of unchecked rage, blue vein twitching on his forehead, that he jumped down from the gate to get on eye level with Emeralda, who was still floating in the air. His red uniform, visor, black chinos, and well-worn leather shoes indicated this was Sadao Maou, but the sheer rage would've given Satan, the Devil King, a run for his money at full strength.

"Is all that holy magic you got on ya just a bunch of fairy dust? Or were you like, '*Oooh*, I'm *soooo* strong, I bet Earth's gonna be *kid* stuff for me!' Well?!!"

"I—I don't know what to saaay..."

Maou's yelling was the only sound in the now utterly silent Shinjuku-sanchome platform. There was no way the station should be this quiet at the seven o'clock hour. Emeralda spotted a large crowd of people behind the platform gates, frozen like stone statues. Maou must have tacked up a barrier of demonic force.

There was little the dejected sorceress could do but take the full brunt of his rage. Out of the corner of her eye, she realized Emi and Laila were floating nearby, in this soundless landscape.

"God*damn*. Chi's got a *lot* more guts than you do. She knows what the words 'risk management' mean, at least. I mean, she launched an Idea Link right when Emi was tossing all that crazy power up and down the Tokyo subway system—and she was *right next* to the battle! You think you could do that for me please?"

"Y-you're riiight... We flew over here because we picked up on Emilia's powerrr release..."

"So Laila had no idea what kind of trouble Emi was in, but she abandoned Nord and didn't say a single word to Suzuno or Ashiya? How dumb can you get?"

"Oof...!"

Emeralda painfully shrugged. Maou was right. As she waited impatiently for Chiho's reply, she had detected a powerful burst of holy force that must have come from Emi. It made her immediately fly off without a second thought. Amane and Laila, picking up on the same burst, joined her midway—but none of them had thought at all about Nord. Perhaps they internally reasoned Shiba could handle anything at their apartment.

"You gotta step it *up*, man," Maou concluded, as if reading her mind. "Chi sent an Idea Link to my and Suzuno's phones, so she

and Ashiya and Urushihara oughtta be guarding Nord now, but...
Ughh."

He snorted, still just barely containing his irritation, before finally removing his eyes from Emeralda. Now he was facing Emi and Laila.

"Just give me...a break... Why is...?"

"Yo, Emi."

"Answer me... Answer me."

"Emi."

"Laila, you..."

"..."

Thrust into the air, surrounded by a barrier of dark energy, Emi was still seething about her mother. Maou wasn't about to wait for her to calm down.

"*Move*, you dumbass."

"Ah?!"

Being pushed in a straight line, parallel to the tracks, by Maou's force was enough to finally make Emi notice his presence. She opened her teary eyes all the way as she looked at Maou. He paid it no mind as he stood next to the unconscious Laila and her pulverized shoulder.

"Man, what in the hell could do *this* to an archangel, huh?" he grumbled to Emeralda—not Emi—as he checked out the wound. "Hey, can we heal this here?"

"N-nooo," she stammered, "not right awaaay. Not in this demon barrier. We need to thoroughly examine her..."

"Okay. I'll do it, then."

"Huh...?"

Before Emeralda could even catch her breath, Maou was focused back on Laila.

"Lemme warn you in advance, I've only used healing magic on nondemons, like, just a few times, and definitely *not* on an angel. If this gets a little hairy, don't come cryin' to me, okay?"

Not even an angel could ignore broken bones and unchecked bleeding for very long before it affected their lives. In fact, considering how astonishingly hardier angels were than your average human-on-the-street, staying alive after this pummeling was a small miracle in itself.

Streams of demonic force began to flow from Maou's fingers. He winced.

"Eesh, what a mess. I thought her shoulder was just smashed in, but it's a lot worse than that. It's like it was hacked to ribbons with a hot knife. How'd the fight get this bad this quick?"

He shot an eyes-only glance at Emi. She remained still, staring blankly into space.

"Nn...hh..."

Whether it was Maou's demonic force doing its work or just the sheer pain of the injury, Laila groaned in her sleep.

"Like, I'm amazed she's not dead from the shock. Healing her's gonna be pretty painful, if it's this bad. Better keep her unconscious for now."

"Maou..."

"Ooh! You all right, Chi? That's good."

Just then, Chiho anxiously walked into the station with Amane.

"I was just in the train the whole time, so... But how's Yusa?"

"She's spacing out over there." He motioned to Emi as he kept up his work. She was floating in space, physically and mentally.

"Seriously, though, what happened?" Maou asked almost to himself as he gave a second glance to Amane.

"He was strong, is what. We let him get away."

Amane attempted a wry smile. But she was hurt. Not as badly as Laila, but hurt. Her long black hair was curled and singed in spots, and her long-sleeved black shirt was torn to shreds, revealing bruises on her skin.

"No way," Maou replied, the fright clear in his voice.

There was little doubting it now, but Amane held the power of the Sephirah, putting her in the same genealogy as Alas Ramus and Acieth. She had utterly dominated Camio, the admittedly elderly Devil's Regent. She brushed the Devil King's full force aside like a passing wind; she made Gabriel retreat without even attempting a fight. And now this new adversary had just severely roughed her up.

Maou checked out Laila's wound, then closed his eyes, trying to imagine what happened. "Well," he said as he ramped up the flow of demonic force to speed up the healing, "guess I'm paying you back now. So *please* don't make me abandon my MgRonald post again, okay?"

"Is Laila hurt?" Chi asked.

"Yesss." Emeralda nodded, not taking her eyes off Maou. "The Devil King is heeealing her." She no longer thought of him as some ruthless, unfeeling monster, but the sight of a demon using his force to *heal* someone was hard to accept. Against most humans, a shot of demonic force was poisonous enough to cause instant sickness. That preconception made her assume any miracle engineered by such force could only work on demons themselves.

It made Emeralda realize that this mere fact—the idea that demons had the concept of healing at all—was enough to jolt her. It painted an all-too-clear picture. All those years fighting them, and she really knew nothing. Maou claimed his force could only heal a certain subset of patients and injuries, and he was probably right. That power was just as harmful to humans as it always was. It would take the constitution of an angel like Laila to survive this treatment.

Then she turned her eyes to Chiho next to her, looking anxiously on at Maou. She was here, in this barrier, close to Maou and all his demonic force, with no protection at all. She must have had a resistance—one she showed back at the hospital room, too, when exposed to enough demon strength to make Nord feel queasy.

"She's... She's become so strong, too...but..."

But what about me?

Maou was right. All this overwhelming power she had at her fingertips, and she still faltered. Just trying to protect a single friend.

"I... I had no idea we were so weak..."

"Nuh-uh." It was Amane who tried to cheer up the repentant

Emeralda, as she watched Maou continue his work. "No point whipping yourself over this, huh? So let's just keep it at that. You guys work at really large scales, so when you screw it up, the fallout's that much bigger, is all. If Chiho can be here for you guys without causing you trouble, that's great, but the same ain't true for you. You have too much power for that. It forces you to deal with a bunch of crap, and when you do, you gotta unleash a ton of power at once."

"Amane…"

"If you're gonna be afraid to make mistakes, you might as well just toss that power in the trash, cover your ears, and live your life alone. And you can't do that, yeah? So…" She turned to Chiho and Maou. "Make up your mind. Like these guys did. Figure out whether you can do it or not, when the time comes."

"Whether I can do it or not…"

"Me, I hate dealing with stuff if I don't have to. Just because I have some power to work with doesn't mean I'm trying to solve every problem in the world. I don't *have* to. It's just, sometimes, I take action so I don't have to regret anything later, like 'if only I did this' or 'if only I did that.' Though…"

Then, something strange happened.

"Just because I take action…that doesn't always mean it turns out right."

The flow of demonic force abated. Maou's treatment was complete. Laila showed no sign of waking up yet, but her breathing was calmer now, the gore around her shoulder completely gone like it had never been. But there were other things happening to her body. Transformations. Things impossible to ignore.

"M-Maou, what's…?"

"Well," a nonplussed Maou said, "if that's what happened to *him*, I guess it's happenin' to *her*, too."

It seemed pretty dramatic to Chiho, despite Maou's deadpan analysis. "Is this," she asked, "like what Sariel talked about? Is she 'fallen' now?"

"I dunno. I don't know what kind of phenomenon being 'fallen' is, really. But I don't think it's anything that drastic."

He shook his head.

"Can I ask a favor, Chi? Can you testify for me that she could've died unless I healed her when I did? 'Cause I have a feeling I'm gonna get a lot of flak for this later. From all sides."

They both meekly looked at Laila as she lay floating in the air, her long, beautiful, silvery hair now a shade of purple.

THE DEVIL
APPRECIATES
THE VALUE OF
MAINTENANCE

Nord, as expected, took it hard.

"Wh-what *happened* to you?! How could this...?!"

By the time Emi and Laila made it back to Villa Rosa Sasazuka—in taxis, with Amane and Emeralda helping them along—they were both thoroughly exhausted and haggard. That, and Laila had just gotten a new hair color.

"Emilia! Are you all right?!"

"..."

Her eyes were too hollow to give a reply.

"What has happened to them?" Nord asked Chiho and Emeralda. The former didn't know where to begin, but before she could, Amane—still propping Laila up on her feet—spoke.

"It's gonna be a long story. Not the sort we'd wanna give outside, either."

She motioned to him to open up Room 101 for the group. "I'll take care of Yusa, so can you help your lady out here?"

"A-ah... Yes... But Laila, too, my goodness..."

The purple hair didn't seem a major concern of his, thankfully, as he took Laila into his arms. Watching them, Emeralda realized that they had all, at that moment, just dodged a bullet. Emi was the first out of the taxi by chance, so Nord naturally turned his attention to her first. If he had given more priority to Laila just now, there was no telling how the Hero might react.

This was an Emi who kept muttering about Laila the whole taxi ride, barely able to keep her eyes in focus. "Why? Why does she try to make my life miserable? Why does she hurt everyone around me? What right does she have?"

"What of the Devil King, Emeralda?" asked Suzuno, freshly relieved from Nord guard duty. Emeralda didn't immediately answer her, taking the time to give the neighborhood of Sasazuka around her a distressed look.

"Ummm… He had to abandon his restauraaant duties to come to us, sooo…"

"Ah. And he has returned to them?"

"Y-yesss."

It flummoxed Emeralda—the idea of this Devil King whirling in to save the day, save an angel's life, then return to his shift without even wrapping anything up—but this was apparently nothing surprising to Suzuno. Suzuno, perhaps out of politeness, did not bring this up with her.

"Indeed, he said their delivery operations would begin shortly. Ms. Kisaki has been out of the office quite a bit, leaving Maou as the shift manager, so to him, it was the only choice to be made."

"Waaas it?"

"Yes. Ask Alciel or Lucifer if you need confirmation. I imagine they will tell you the same. I doubt Chiho found it unusual, either, no? And Amane was more than capable of ferrying them back here by herself, as you saw."

"C-cerrrtainly," Emeralda murmured, wide-eyed at how accurately Suzuno painted the picture despite her absence.

"Interact with your neighbors as much as I have, and you learn quickly."

"Ahh…"

"But regardless. You had best rest up for now, Emeralda, and let me know if anything happens. It must have been a dreadful battle. I could feel Emilia's force all the way from here."

"I wasn't there for the whole show myselllf," Emeralda mused as she crossed her arms. "I'm not sure it's fair to even call it a baaattle. And Emilia herself, well…"

"…Yes." Suzuno nodded, looking at Emi as she beckoned them to join her in Room 101. "Something terrible must have happened."

"She was griping about Laila the whole taxi ride hooome. In this real low, scaaary voice."

"Not an encouraging trend, no."

Suzuno wasn't aware that Emi had abandoned her apartment for three days, but she knew Emi had been trying to banish Laila from her mind as of late, a move she respected a great deal. The results, however, had proven less than favorable.

The moment they opened the door to Room 101, Emi froze, looked up, and practically leaped backward, almost bowling over Nord and Chiho.

"Emilia?!"

"Yusa?"

"I'm not going in."

"Huh?"

"I can't be in the same room as that woman."

"Quit your worrying," a bewildered Amane said. "You already got a Devil King in this joint. What could be worse?"

Emi turned her hollow, exhausted eyes upward. "I'll wait upstairs."

"Upstairs?"

"In *his* room!!" she shouted half-hysterically, dragging Chiho by the arm as she walked off. "I don't want to listen to Laila! I don't *care* what's happening wherever! I usually wait upstairs with Alas Ramus! For the Devil King and Chiho to come back! And I'm gonna do that now, too! You all just do whatever you want!!"

"Y-Yusa, um, um, agh," Chiho said as Emi almost lifted her by the arm to the second floor.

"Alciel! Lucifer! I'm coming in!!"

"You may, if you wish, but if you are shameless enough to ask for dinner as well, help me prepare the peas. Feel free to sit down, Ms. Sasaki; I am sure you are tired."

"Dude, you could at least act like you're sorry for bothering us."

Ashiya and Urushihara were enough used to Emi's sudden intrusions that they offered no further objection. In another moment, the front door to Room 201 was slammed shut, so forcefully that Ashiya feared she would smash it to pieces.

"......" Nord watched all this unfold, unable to speak. Amane just shrugged. "Boy, she sure hates her, huh? What a drag," she said, not looking at all concerned.

Emeralda, meanwhile, drooped her shoulders down like an abandoned puppy.

"Emiliaaa..."

"I apologize, Emeralda," Suzuno said, patting the dejected sorceress on the shoulder, "but would you mind waiting in my apartment? Given that you were there to witness this evening's events, you going inside to see Laila might be too much for Emilia to bear."

"...Yesss, all right."

"Understand, I am sure you still have Emilia's trust, Emeralda."

"Oh, I knowww, it's just... Well, it's too late to do much about nowww, I suppose. You can take me out of Ente Isla, but you can't take Ente Isla out of meee, you could say. My presence must push all her 'Heeero' buttons, mmm?"

She looked up the stairs leading to Villa Rosa Sasazuka's second floor, eyes saddened but not wet with tears.

"Right nowww, she's 'Emi Yusa,' isn't sheee? And Emi Yusa's problems need to be solved heeere, with all her friends in Japaaan. I'm here to supporrrt her, no matter whaaat decision she maaakes."

"Indeed, Japan is a rather...more comfortable place to be than I expected. Perhaps you should consider an extended stay as well, Emeralda."

"I doubt my government post would allowww that. And no matter how easy it is in Japan, how nice the food is, I still feel more at hooome in Saint Aile."

"Do you?"

Suzuno nodded and smiled before giving Emeralda the key to her front door. "If you wouldn't mind staying there while I run a quick errand? If you need a drink, help yourself to anything in the refrigerator."

"…Well, come back sooon," Emeralda said as she accepted it. "I always feel awwwkward about puttering around in someone else's paaantry."

"I will." Suzuno gave Emeralda a light hug, along with a few affectionate pats on the back. "Amane, if you wouldn't mind…"

"You want me to guard? Sure, sure," came the listless reply. "Guess we got Ashiya and Urushihara upstairs, not to mention Emeralda. Not like things'll break bad *that* fast if someone shows up."

Suzuno nodded at this, then briskly took her leave, walking away from the apartment. The phone told her it was just before eight.

"A little junk food for dinner now and then is hardly a bad thing," she whispered as she strode off toward the center of Sasazuka.

"Hmm?"

The moment the front doors at the MgRonald by Hatagaya station whirred open, Suzuno spotted two familiar faces in the corner of her eye. She turned toward them. They gave her a little wave.

"Rika?"

"Hey," Rika Suzuki said from the sofa-style seating lining the wall.

"And…Acieth?"

Across from her was Acieth Alla, looking supremely satisfied with the small mountain of paper wrappings on the table. Despite appearing roughly the age of a middle schooler, she was Alas Ramus's younger sister, another personification of a Yesod fragment—what was she doing hanging in MgRonald, with Rika?

"Ooh! Suzuno! I am the very, very full!"

"I imagine so. And I do hope you did not force Rika here to pay for an order of this magnitude."

To someone like Suzuno, who didn't partake in fast food all that often, the number of burger wrappings in front of Acieth—not to mention the four paper cups surrounding them—seemed utterly bizarre.

She seemed unlikely to have enough to pay for this herself. Suzuno feared for the hapless Rika, forced to shell out just because they happened to know each other.

"Well, funny thing about that," Rika said, a twinge of resignation in her voice as she grinned and picked up one of the wrappings. "She said that this lady, Ms. Shiba, will repay me if I give her the receipt."

This made Suzuno bring a hand to her face. She looked upward, seeking divine guidance for this wild child before her. "If Maou was not on duty," she remarked, "I rather believe he would sock you on the head again."

"Aww, so mean! Maou, he is so quick with the violence to me! It is big drag!"

"But that is not the point. The point is that it's disgraceful to be so reliant on other people's money like that. I would expect that from Lucifer, but not you."

"Heh. I feel kinda bad about Urushihara getting scapegoated like that." Rika, well versed in the affairs of Maou and his kin, already knew Urushihara's real name. "But ah, well. It's all right, Suzuno. Ms. Shiba's the landlord at your apartment, right? If she sees Emi and Maou a lot, I'm bound to run into her, so I'll bring it up then."

"…My apologies, Rika. I will be sure to give Shiba a piece of my mind about it."

It was nothing for Suzuno to apologize about, but Shiba *did* tend to oddly spoil her acquaintances. It was generous of her, one could say, but Suzuno was starting to think she just had very poor spending habits.

"But what brings you two here tonight?"

"Probably the same reason you're here, Suzuno."

Rika showed her a news site on her phone. It had all the latest info on the mystery accident that took place in the Tokyo Metro Fukutoshin Line a bit ago.

"One of the newer staffers at Dokodemo lives off the Fukutoshin Line," she explained, scowling a bit as she put her phone away. "In Zoshigaya. Her name's Maki, and like, she's totally crazy for Emi, you know? And she was like, 'Oh, I'm so worried, I'm so worried,' so I figured I'd come here just to make sure it's nothing too hairy. If it's Ente Isla stuff, Maou's bound to get involved anyway, so. And if it's nothing, then—hey—I'll just have a little 'cheat' dinner here. But on the way here, I tried contacting Emi, and she didn't answer my phone calls or texts."

Judging by the shape Emi was in, Suzuno surmised it would be a while before she cared about her phone.

"So," Rika continued, voice growing quieter, "by sheer coincidence, I ran into Maou and Acieth in front of the MgRonald here."

"Not that I *wants* to come," Acieth mumbled, eyebrows down. "Maou, he had to go out of Hatagaya, so I forced to fuse with him. And we go to subway, and ohh, so angry, so angry! Nothing I can poke the fun at."

This suggested that Acieth's typically bubbleheaded observations were a deliberate act, to some extent, but that didn't matter right now.

"So you saw what happened in Shinjuku, Acieth?"

"Yes, starting in middle. *Uhhhrrp!*"

The titanic belch that emanated from the Yesod fragment personification, a girl in the blooming stages of her life, was followed by her nodding and rubbing her belly.

"Amane and Chiho, they are home?"

"Yes, just a moment ago."

"And Emi and Eme together?"

Rika sat up at the question, looking at Suzuno.

"Yes, they are all at Villa Rosa Sasazuka at the moment…" Suzuno hedged.

…*Though it is a difficult situation to explain.*

"…But Emilia is even more repulsed by the presence of Laila than she was before," she finished. "She may not even be willing to reason with Emeralda right now."

Rika winced. "Ooh, did something bad happen to her again?"

"I have no details yet. She and Emeralda both looked shocked and exhausted to me, and I need Amane to keep an eye on Laila and guard the apartment for us. Thus, I thought I would discuss matters with the Devil King once I had a spare moment..."

She looked around the dining space.

"...But he is not here. Is he upstairs, or in the back?"

"He went somewhere with that pretty manager after he wrapped up Acieth's order."

"Hmm. Hopefully he is not being rebuked for leaving to help Emilia. But I cannot loiter in here without ordering anything. Would you mind if I sat with you?"

"Ooh! Is okay for round two?!"

"Acieth, are you listening to us? I thought you said you were full just now."

Leaving her goldfish-print tote bag with the exasperated Rika, Suzuno took out her wallet and walked up to the counter, currently manned by a burly gentleman.

"Hello! Let me know when you're ready to order!"

"Umm..." She looked at the menu. It was a daunting task. "If I could order this Full-Moon Burger meal...er, medium size?"

"Certainly," the man replied, bringing his hand to the drink menu to aid the clearly confused Suzuno. "What kind of drink would you like? The selections in red cost an extra hundred yen."

"Errr, hot coffee, please."

"Would you like milk and sugar with that?"

"No sugar. Just the milk."

"All right. So just to confirm your order..."

This order-taking business was making sweat form around her forehead. This was, she realized, the first time she had ever gone into a MgRonald and ordered by herself. She usually visited with Emi, and if not, then either Maou or Chiho were usually behind the counter, so there normally wasn't much to be nervous about. She was at least acquainted with Kisaki, the manager, as well—but ordering with a stranger like this made her muse about just how unused to MgRonald she really was. She only ordered the Full-Moon Burger because it was at the top of the menu, a limited-time item, and because it had an unusual name. She knew nothing about it.

"I see there is much for me to learn, still..."

And this was how she acted as a customer. If she were an employee? No, there was no way she could handle this dizzying array of food items. It made her sigh a little as she took out a thousand-yen bill, before realizing that, as she received her change, the cashier was looking right into her eyes.

"Um...?"

"Oh, er, sorry. You know Marko...I mean, Maou, don't you?"

"I do," the bemused Suzuno replied, "but how did you know?" She took another look at the employee. His face didn't ring a bell.

"How, well..." The large man scratched the side of his head. "I just remembered that I've seen you in here with Maou a few times. That, and with Yusa before she got hired. And you know, seeing a young woman in a kimono when it's not during a festival or something made you kind of stand out in my mind, so... Sorry if I'm being weird."

"Oh, not at all, but...hmm. Perhaps I should expand my wardrobe a tad."

She had been semi-forced into more modern clothing for Emi's birthday party, but Suzuno liked what she liked, and that outfit was now stuffed deep into a closet. Taking a look at the man's name tag, it said KAWATA in capital letters.

"Maou's in the back office for the time being, but I think he'll return in a bit. I'll tell him to stop by your seat when he does. Here's your Full-Moon Burger and coffee set."

"Ah, thank you," Suzuno said, regaining her composure. "Hmmm..."

She couldn't help but feel a little out of sorts as she turned around and headed for Rika's table, gaze pointed at her feet.

"What's up?" Rika asked.

"Oh, er, I was just thinking about how my choice of clothing might be a tad too conspicuous."

"Uh, duh?" Rika giggled. "I mean, I've known you long enough that I couldn't imagine you in anything else, but…"

"You think so? Hmmm… I do have some more sensible long-sleeved wear for the winter, but perhaps I should consider a more varied Western wardrobe… Ah, but look at me." She shook her head, attempting to banish the subject from her mind. "Enough about my clothing. What about Emilia? Acieth, what happened to… Um. Hello?"

Her face stiffened before she could finish the question.

"Yeah, uh, she's been that way ever since you stood up to place that order."

"Nngggggguuuuhhhh…"

Acieth, fresh from gorging herself on someone else's tab, was now slumped back on one of the plastic chairs bolted to the table, snoring loudly as she enjoyed her post-meal siesta.

"Ugh, has she no sense of urgency at all?!"

She had just been witness, in sword form, to epoch-making events—events that thoroughly thrashed Emi and Emeralda and didn't even leave Amane unscathed. Yet, here she was. Everyone knew she wasn't the type to think too deeply about matters as a rule, but this was just too much.

"Acieth! Wake up! No sleeping allowed in the dining hall!"

"Mngh…"

Suzuno grabbed her arms and began shaking. She didn't open her eyes.

"Nuu…ahm…I—I can eat still…"

"I was not asking you that!"

"Boy, looking at that, it makes you wonder if anything serious happened after all, huh? I almost feel silly worrying about it."

"Do not let her deceive you, Rika! This is just Acieth's personality at work—it must be more serious than this! Come on, Acieth!"

"Urh…nnffffuuu…"

"Maybe we oughtta let her be until Maou comes back?"

"Alas Ramus cares so much about her parents! Why must you be so different from her?!"

"Maybe it was just her environment, or upbringing or something? I mean, Alas Ramus is just the cutest li'l angel right now, but maybe she'll wind up more like this eventually?"

"I refuse to let that happen! Acieth! Acieth, get up!"

She couldn't be too loud, not wanting to alarm the other diners in the room. But right now, Suzuno's top priority in life was to get this glutton back into the realm of the conscious.

Maou chose that moment to return from the staff room.

"Whewwww... Man, I thought she was gonna ream me out."

He had zoomed right back to MgRonald after healing Laila and leaving her in Amane's hands. When he did, Rika was waiting out front—and Kisaki was waiting inside. He had expected his manager to be working at the regional office all day, so the mere sight of her was enough to make Maou shrink back in terror. Luckily, Kisaki didn't bring up his absence at all; she just wanted to go over the things that needed to be done on tomorrow's shift.

"You owe us one for that," Kawata commented, deliberately looking as annoyed as possible at him. "I mean, deciding to take off for half an hour while we're getting slammed? What was up with that?"

"Sorry, Kawatchi. I'll make up for it, okay? What'd you say to Ms. Kisaki?"

"Well, you said you'd be back in half an hour, yeah? Ms. Kisaki showed up five minutes before you did, Marko, so I took your word for it and told her you ran out to deliver a forgotten item back to a customer. But, *man*, was I spooked! Next time, tell me what you're out doing, at least!"

"Sure thing," Maou said as he put his hands together and gave Kawata an apologetic bow.

"No worries. But what were you talking about back there? Why the big meeting just to talk about tomorrow?"

"Oh, well, we're gonna take delivery tomorrow on our fleet of scooters, but it's kind of dicey whether Ms. Kisaki's gonna be here on time for the drop-off, so she wanted to brief me on the procedure just in case."

"Oh, that! It's almost time, huh? Makes me a little nervous."

It had been just over two months since the MagCafé space opened upstairs, and now the franchise was diving headlong into their delivery program. The period between now and when Kisaki made the first announcement was, to say the least, a *packed* time in Maou's life. It felt far longer than just two months in his mind, what with the arrival of Acieth and Nord, his journey to Ente Isla, and—most daunting of all—Emi both joining the Mag's crew and dealing with mommy drama.

For the Lord of All Demons, these were quite literally world-altering events, all stuffed into a scant few weeks. But it didn't mean great changes in the life of Maou himself. He had his demonic force back, and being fused with Acieth gave him the power to explore the Sephirah's secrets in depth, but it didn't alter his goals at all. Even having Emi closer to him than ever was something he found easy enough to sidestep—her less-than-rosy opinion of him was no surprise by now.

Over in his native realm, and over on Ente Isla as well, things had stabilized a fair bit. The heavens had shut itself out from the rest of the universe. There shouldn't have been anything happening to cause Maou any trouble. But then today came along—which meant there was a troublemaker in their midst, or at least a new risk they had been overlooking up to now.

Even if they *had* overlooked it, though, it seemed to be mostly Emi's problem in his mind. Nothing much, Maou thought, that had to do with him, really. Hence, he saw no reason to go out of his way to seek out new risks. It was just a waste of time, and it wouldn't bring anything good. Right now, the most important thing was to work with the crew he trusted to get this new delivery program off on the right foot.

"Oh, by the way, Marko…"

"Hmm? …Hey, what are you looking at me like that for?"

The weirdly sharp eyes of Kawata daunted him.

"You got some friends here."

"Friends?"

"Yeah. That girl in the kimono who's always here with Yusa or Chi. Table thirty-one."

His gaze darted toward the table. There he saw the backs of Rika's and Suzuno's heads as they sat primly on the sofa seat, Acieth sprawled out in an uncomfortable-looking position across from them.

"Oh, yeah, Suzuno. Boy, I hope she ain't gonna interrogate me the way Rika Suzuki did."

Emi and the others were likely back at Villa Rosa Sasazuka by now. Suzuno must be here to grill Maou on today's events.

"Man, Maou. I mean, like, *really*? You already got Chi, and *now* look at all the chicks you're haulin' in here. That one girl isn't even from Japan, is she? And what about that lady in the office outfit?"

"Q-quit making it weird, Kawata. It's nothing that fancy. Suzuno's just my neighbor, Acieth's kind of a distant relative, and that other lady's friends with Emi and Chi, mostly. And quit name-checking Chi like that, too. I swear, it's nothing yet!"

"Yet. *Yet.* Plus, you gotta be kidding me; what's a proper-looking girl like that kimono chick doing living in the same crappy apartment as a single guy like you? That has to be, like, an urban legend."

"Oh, thanks for reviewing my apartment for me, Kawatchi. Plus, I'm not single. I told you, I'm sharing the place with two of my friends."

"*Male* friends? You? Yeah, right."

"Eesh."

Kawata was likely just picking on him, he knew. But then his coworker took another look at Suzuno at table thirty-one, eyes resolute.

"I dunno, though; that lady looks pretty worked up about something. I've never seen her come in by herself to see you before. Something bad didn't happen to Chi or Yusa or something, did it?"

"…"

Maou was stricken by the paranoid delusion that Kawata actually knew everything about him and Ente Isla. That was *exactly* what Suzuno was here for—but it couldn't have been so easily deducible by Kawata, not unless he knew about Emi's plans the way Rika did. In the mere ten or so minutes Maou was with Kisaki in the back, Kawata had observed Suzuno, a woman he knew nothing about, and stumbled upon the correct conclusion.

"Y'know," Maou suggested, "you should really reconsider your career path, man. Your parents can run that restaurant for a little while longer, can't they? If you don't wanna be a therapist, then think about being a teacher or something—but either way, Kawatchi, you really oughtta find a job where you're dealing with people more."

"You deal with people all the time at a restaurant," Kawata countered, and the conversation ended there. Kawata had his duties, and Maou was due to be manning the café's cash register.

"Oof," he muttered, noticing the guests at table thirty-one looking at him and trying to ignore it. "If you're waiting for me, do it at home." Then he tried going upstairs. He tried, but he didn't make it.

"Uggghhhh…"

Turning around, he headed for table thirty-one.

"…Um, madam, could you please refrain from sleeping here?"

"Ooo…I'm…hungry."

Acieth was bent backward on her seat, sleeping peacefully, her stomach area very clearly bulging out a little. It must've been quite a dream she was having.

"Hey, Rika, did this girl *really* just eat forty burgers by herself?"

"She kinda hit a wall at thirty-five," Rika commented. "She wants to take the rest home, though."

"If she can eat that much, she really oughtta go all the way, man." Maou shrugged. "I'm on closing duty today, and I can't get out early from that. You should head on home once you're done eating; you're gonna miss the last train."

"Rika," Suzuno said, "you can stay in my apartment if you like.

It is not very spacious, but I do have all the toiletries and such you would need."

"Are you listening to me?" Maou stammered, lips trembling. "It's not like anything *that* major happened. This weird dude attacked the subway train Emi and Chi were riding on; Amane and Laila swung in to help; Laila got hurt; and then I healed her. That's all."

Rika's eyebrows twitched as she checked out the news on her phone. The reports stated that the cause of the stoppage and subsequent bizarre events were a complete unknown so far. Nobody was injured, but three out of the subway's ten cars were derailed, two of them showing evidence of their doors being pried open by force. The connection between the conductor's "person on the tracks" and the emergency-stop button being activated in Shinjuku-sanchome Station was still unclear, and since it had only been a couple hours since the incident, the Fukutoshin Line still wasn't running trains at all. The assorted privately owned rail lines that piggybacked onto that line were now a total mess.

"Laila was already hurt by the time I received Chi's Idea Link and ran over. I sealed off the area around Shinjuku-sanchome with a barrier just because I figured it could've been a pretty crappy situation. And my demonic healing changed Laila's hair color, I guess, but it sure as hell beats havin' her die on my watch, doesn't it? And really, that's just about all I can tell you. So finish up your dinner, relax as long as you want, and then get outta here, all right?"

The fact Maou didn't tell them to leave right this moment struck Suzuno and Rika as a token attempt at politeness. But neither was particularly satisfied.

"And who," Suzuno asked, "is this so-called weird dude who attacked? Whoever it was proved a worthy adversary for Amane, no less!"

"Amane?" Rika asked. "That's the dark-haired lady who helped me a while back, isn't it? I should've known she wasn't, like, normal..."

"I told you guys, I don't know! Emi was in too much of a panic to explain anything to me, and Emeralda said she only saw a coupla glimpses or whatever. We didn't exactly have a lotta time to talk. So really, you'd learn a hell of a lot more from Chi and Amane than you would from me right now."

"Um…how *is* Emi? After all, um…?"

"If that's how you're puttin' it, I guess you heard about her, huh? It's a total mess of a mother-daughter relationship. Her dad's one thing, but Emi and her mom just do not get along, man. It's nothing that anyone on the outside can do anything about. I gotta get back to work, okay? Have fun for now. Also, can you get Acieth out of her stupor for me? Thanks."

"Wait, um…"

Ignoring Rika's plea, Maou tromped upstairs without a second glance.

"Well, that was cold," she wistfully groaned.

"…"

Suzuno simply began tackling her fries, opting against trying to force anything further out of Maou.

"What should we do, Suzuno? Wait 'til he gets off? 'Cause he totally sounds like he's hiding something."

"You saw that as well?"

"Huh? Um…I guess?" Rika cocked an eyebrow at Suzuno, grinning at her as she methodically picked up one fry at a time and elegantly nibbled upon it.

"The Devil King is providing us with needless detail while dancing around the crux of it all. This crux, however, is not directly related to current events, so I could not press him on it. If I did, he would be stubborn as a mule about it."

"Oh? What d'you mean?"

"Hmm, hmm, hmm." Suzuno took a sip of coffee and looked back at the stairs. "How long, exactly, did the Devil King leave the restaurant?"

"Hmm?"

"I heard him speaking with the gentleman behind the counter just now."

"Y-you could hear that? Over there?" Rika looked toward the

counter. It was located a healthy distance away from their table. The dining hall was maybe three-fifths full now, but even if Rika strained her ears, there was no way she could decipher the heavyset man at the register.

"A side effect of my work experience," Suzuno explained. "Maou said he would be back in half an hour. It seems he followed through on that promise, but if he only took action after receiving Chiho's SOS, that is a breathtakingly narrow window of time to work with. Plus…"

"Plus?"

"Forgive me for asking, Rika, but does your workplace allow you to carry your personal phone with you at the office?"

"Huh? You mean, can I use my phone at work? No, they kinda frown upon that."

"Right. Personal phone use is prohibited while one is on duty. So when, exactly, do you think the Devil King noticed the Idea Link from Chiho?"

"Um, what was an Idea Link again? Like, some kind of ESP magic from your world, right?"

"Indeed. Chiho went through a, shall we say, accelerated program to learn how to use it."

"Heh. Little after-school work, huh?"

Suzuno ignored this. "Chiho is not a sorceress. She is merely operating upon the powers that have been forcibly instilled into her; she cannot tap into such magic empty-handed. Thus, she uses her mobile phone as a tool to aid her in the spell."

She gave a concise explanation of the phone's role as an amplifier for the magic required to craft an Idea Link. Rika had first heard about this skill from Chiho herself, but receiving the full rundown from a native Ente Islan made her realize how exceptional Chiho was all over again.

"Boy, the way you're explaining it, you make it sound like Chiho's got these weird voices in her head all the time."

"Yes, well, regardless, without her mobile phone handy, Chiho's

Idea Link signals will never reach their destination. When the attack took place, the Devil King was busily attending to the dinner rush here—and yet, he received the Idea Link and rushed to the scene. What do you think that means?"

"Hmm? Umm..." Rika racked her brain, not grasping Suzuno's point at first. "Was he just on break? Probably not, huh? Not right in the middle of dinner. And I can't really picture Maou hiding a phone on him during work—or anyone here, really. Umm... I give up. What is it?"

"Simple. The Devil King had already left the building before receiving Chiho's signal. ...This Full-Moon Burger is rather more difficult to eat than I expected."

"Huh?"

Unwrapping the burger, Suzuno was clearly startled at the odd thickness to it. It was a lot for her small lips to wrap themselves around.

"Mm...ph... She ate thirty-five of those, you say? What is her stomach composed of, I wonder?"

She looked at Acieth, perplexed.

"But the holy force within Emilia is nothing like what a normal person holds. When paired with Alas Ramus, it is no exaggeration to say that she is the strongest human being in the universe, save for special cases like Shiba or Amane."

"In the *universe*, huh?" Rika giggled.

"We cannot say what kind of enemy attacked us, but Emilia fought it off with her holy sword. Hearing the sounds of combat, Chiho realized there was no way of escaping this and used her Idea Link skills—and the Devil King immediately received it. Which means that the Devil King must've flown out of this restaurant when he detected Emilia's holy magic in action. *That* is why he was there to pick up the Idea Link the moment it arrived."

"...Okay, but so what, then? That doesn't sound weird at all to me."

It didn't. Maou felt Emi engaged in combat, realized something urgent was going on, and took off. Nothing questionable about that.

"No, perhaps it would not be to you, Rika. But to us, this is a serious issue... Oof, even one of these is too much for me. I wish there were some vegetables to go with this, or at least some green tea."

Given her normally healthy, austere eating habits, tucking into your typical MgRonald combo meal was, perhaps, going way too far toward the other end of the spectrum. She gave a quizzical look at the meal she had finished up in a scant few minutes.

"But Sadao Maou is the Devil King, and Emilia is the Hero. They remain enemies, just as much now as before. But when he detected Emilia's fighting force in action, the Devil King ran out of this MgRonald even before Chiho's SOS arrived. You do not see the enormity of this?"

"Meaning, he left here because he thought Emi was in danger?"

Suzuno firmly nodded. "To the Devil King of once upon a time, it would be unthinkable."

The Maou of just a bit ago, freshly settled in Sasazuka, never would. Chiho and Suzuno could plead at him all they wanted; he would brush it all off. *Emi's problems are hers, not mine. I'm busy with work. She's the Hero; let her work it out.* That wasn't necessarily the case if Chiho was also endangered, but Maou only knew about Chiho's presence after he already decided to ditch work.

"This has been a trend as of late," Suzuno observed as she neatly folded up the burger wrapper, "and it has been growing more striking by the day. He may gripe and groan about Emilia, but the Devil King truly thinks of her as a valued companion. He did once declare Emilia a Great Demon General, if more to talk his way out of a tight spot than anything, but I feel that is starting to take hold in his mind, in a very real way."

"Hmm... Hmmmmm?"

Rika struggled to digest this roundabout argument.

"So you mean..."

Then the natural conclusion struck her.

"That...wait, that... *Huh?*"

"Quite a surprise, yes?" Suzuno clapped her hands, grateful that Rika now shared the same thought as she did. "Considering the nature of their relationship."

"Well, yeah, it sure is! So it's like..."

"Yes?"

"It's like Emi's a girl Maou feels like he's got to *protect* now?!"

".....................Er?"

Her smile froze at this unexpected development, eyebrows gradually wandering up her forehead.

"Well, um, no, I just mean, oh geez, it's like, you know, *that*, isn't it? Like, through all the antagonism, some kinda forbidden love rearing its head... Heeee! It's just so steamy to think about!!"

"Sa...say again?"

"That's what you mean, right? They've been enemies for so long, but now that they're together, they're starting to feel things besides hatred for each other, and now Maou's become aware of it, right?"

"Mmmm?! Wait! Rika?! I—I do not feel that is correct! I do not!"

"Well, I sure do! They're so bonded together now that he, like, reflexively worries about Emi at this point!"

"I do not...feel...that is correct, perhaps, but that is not the point here!"

"Oh, don't worry about it, Suzuno! It's not like I'm tryin' to pair them together or anything!"

"Then why are you grinning so ominously like that?!"

"Awww, you knowwwwww!" Rika was now beaming, the furrowed brows a thing of the past. "It's easier to make relationships simple like that, y'know? To keep things easy to understand!"

"Huh?"

"I mean, with Emi and Maou, we know she's the human Hero and he's the king of demons. But in between that, there were all those other elements, right? Like, 'my sworn enemy,' 'murderer of my parents,' 'razer of my lands,' and stuff?"

"I—I suppose, yes."

"And those are all *huge* obstacles! Like, nothing you could ever overcome, usually, right? But y'know, from Maou's perspective, he's already cleared 'em all, hasn't he? I mean, the moment he thought that maybe Emi was in danger, he might've been sprinting for the door right then 'n' there, huh?"

Rika was correct, certainly. But this wasn't exactly the conversation Suzuno intended to have. And there was something in her heart that was too eager to accept the concept for her tastes. She briskly shook her head.

"N-no, but… It may be that way to the Devil King, but I see no evidence that Emilia has taken any special steps toward him…"

"Whatcha getting worked up for, Suzuno?"

"Wh-what? I am not…'worked up' over…"

"Your face is all red, though."

"Ah?!" She touched her cheek. It didn't tell her what color it was. "N-no, I…"

"Hmm… Though it makes sense, maybe. You aren't like Chiho— you're from Ente Isla, so the idea of the Devil King gettin' close with the Hero isn't necessarily the happiest news in the world, huh?"

"N-no. It is not—not at…"

Or was it?

She immediately latched on to Rika's hypothesis, but the moment the words flew out, the cold, reasoning part of her mind warned her that she didn't think that one bit. She *had* to latch on to Rika—she had no other choice, given that she never thought otherwise up to now. But Rika, not noticing the emotions churning inside Suzuno, gave her a world-beating smile.

"Wow, though, huh? Imagine! The two of them, coming to terms!"

"Nh, um, well, yes, that may be the case, but…"

"Don't you think that's wonderful?"

"…………………………………………………Er?"

Rika rested her chin on both hands. "Like I said, I'm not expecting Emi and Maou to start dating or anything…"

"N-no…"

"But you know, it's awkward to see two of your friends continually butt heads against each other, isn't it? I think I'm starting to understand how Chiho feels a little. Like, how nice it'd be if people and demons can get by without having to kill one another."

"Rika..."

She chuckled a bit, embarrassed at herself. "Plus, it's like, 'me too,' so..."

"Hmm?"

"...I dunno, I just really feel I get Chiho now. Like, painfully so. And I get how Chiho can stand so firm while all this stuff happens around her. I'm kinda surprised to say this, but it doesn't bother me at all that those guys are demons or whatever. It's just...compared to Chiho, I don't really think there's anything, like, *going* on in that way, for me..."

Rika paused, then slumped over the table, next to the tray.

"I just don't think we're *ever* gonna go phone shopping."

"Phone shopping?"

Suzuno tilted her head at this sudden swerve.

"It's nothing," Rika said, voice stonier than she expected as she got over herself and sat up. "Think I might as well head on home. At least I know what's going on now. I'm just glad I heard about Emi—if she's that worked up, I better not stick my head in quite yet, but... Huh?"

Now her head was turned to the seat across from her.

"Where'd Acieth go?"

"Hmm?!"

Suzuno, surprised, looked over herself. Acieth had been draped all over her chair just a moment ago, deep into ever-greedier dreams, and now she was gone.

"It is still warm," she remarked upon touching the chair. "I don't think she could be that far. The bathroom, perhaps?"

"No, I got a feeling this is something...bad..."

Rika stopped as she heard someone stomping down the MgRonald stairwell. She whipped around to look.

Sadao Maou was there, the smile lashed to his face only barely hiding a fearsome torrent of anger as he walked. Once down the stairs, he strode right up to Suzuno and Rika, still smiling as he spoke in a voice that welled up from the deepest pits of hell—a truly Satan-like performance.

"*What* have you guys been telling Acieth?"

"…Huh?"

"Me and Emi are *what*, exactly?"

"Gehh!"

"Nnnnh—!"

Rika almost yelped out a groan as Suzuno slumped down, hand over her forehead. They were so caught up in conversation that they failed to notice, but Acieth was already awake by the time Rika's theorizing reached its climax. Neither of them noticed her presence at all. Did Acieth do that on purpose? Whether she did or not, she must've zoomed right up those stairs and given Maou the full executive summary, in her own words.

"N-no, listen, Devil King, this was just a figure of speech…"

"Save your speeches for the leeches, you dumbass. Whether you're joking or not, *some* things are better left unsaid, y'know."

"B-but it's a good thing, Maou! Like, helping out your enemies… You're, like, the very model of a Devil King! It's really cool of ya!"

"If you want to praise me, you could at least look me in the eye."

"You-you're really great, Devil King! Let's give 'im a round of applause!"

"Suzuno, if you go *that* far out of character, you're gonna regret it in a flash."

"I will keep that in mind!" the cherry-red Suzuno replied in a panic. "I *already* rather regret it!!"

"Um, where's Acieth?"

"Inside." Maou pointed at his head. "I swear, if I don't put a leash around her neck, there's seriously no telling what she'll say or do. She's a thousand times worse than Emi that way, that dolt."

His face twisted in irritation the moment he said the word "dolt." Acieth was no doubt shouting her objections to this doglike treatment.

"…You guys should be really happy Ms. Kisaki was here today. It's thanks to her that I can bottle up all this anger. You done talking now?"

"Y-yes," the docile Rika and Suzuno echoed.

"Let me take your tray for you. See you next time."

They both detected more than a hint of the Lord of All Demons in the face of Sadao Maou, fast-food employee, as they hurried out.

"You would call that 'coming to terms'?" remarked a depressed Suzuno as they approached Hatagaya station.

"I'm not so confident any longer, no…"

"…Oh. Oh, dear," Suzuno said abruptly.

"What?"

Suzuno winced while Rika was fumbling through her handbag for her train pass.

"I meant to tell the Devil King something, and I forgot. And yet, he will be at work until the early hours…"

"Oh? Well, I dunno what it is, but he'd probably kick us out if we came back. Why don't you text it to him?"

"I suppose I will have to."

Suzuno took out her phone, slowly tapping with an unpracticed hand.

"This will do…"

Her message finally typed out, she read over it again to ensure there were no errors. But just as her finger wavered over the SEND icon, she froze.

"………………………………………………………………………………
……………………"

"Uh, why'd you stop?" Rika asked, concerned over the way Suzuno suddenly acted like a windup doll with no windup left.

"This is the first time, is it not?" she murmured as the gears slowly went back into motion.

"What is?"

"Oh, er, nothing important. I just realized, after all this time living next door, this is the first time I have texted the Devil King."

She *did* have his phone number, something she had extracted from him long ago just in case. But despite their positions in the battle over Ente Isla, they saw each other practically every day anyway. If they had business with each other, it was easier to just yell through the windows than bother with texting. The whole concept never even occurred to her until just the other day—just before he headed off for Ente Isla in search of Emi. She paused again.

"......"

"Um, what's up, Suzuno? Was it that sketchy a topic you forgot to bring up?"

"N-no, not exactly, but..."

Rika raised an eyebrow at her friend's irresolute behavior. She looked a bit inconsolable, even, as she shook her head.

"It just seems like such a...silly thing to send my first text to him about."

She began tapping away again, editing the message on her screen, using features on her phone that she normally never used with Emi and Chiho.

"*So* silly," she concluded as she pressed the SEND button. Once it sent, she turned off the screen and looked back at Rika.

"If I may be honest, I cannot say what exactly transpired today. But once I do know, in detail, I promise I will contact you, Rika. I hope you will be patient until then."

"Sure thing. I dunno how much I can help, but if you wanna hold a 'let's cheer up Emi' party or whatever, I'll be happy to emcee. Have a good one! Say hi to everyone."

"Certainly. Have a safe journey."

Rika waved and disappeared into Hatagaya station. Once she did, Suzuno turned around and began walking back to the apartment.

"Go out of character, and you will instantly regret it. Even I know that much."

She took out her phone and opened her message history. Mostly, it was full of conversations with Chiho and Emi, but now DEVIL KING was on the very top. She read over the message once more before breezily strolling through the Sasazuka night back home.

"Hey, Marko?"

It was nine in the evening. Suzuno and Rika were gone, and a burger binge had made the fused Acieth settle back down into a resentful sleep. Maou had just hit the staff room to add the latest sales journal to the account books when Kisaki spoke up.

"Yes?"

"I heard something heavy fall inside your locker just now. Maybe your phone or your wallet fell out of your pocket?"

"Ooh, really?"

"It was really loud, too. It startled me a bit. You better check it out to make sure nothing broke."

"Sure, um, thanks."

Hurrying over to his locker, he found the brand-new phone that Emi had just brought him lying on the bottom. It was an older flip-top model, the kind with a small screen on the rear of the device, and it was lit up to alert him about a new text. The vibration from the text alert probably made it fall out.

Reflexively, he opened it up—only to find a message from Suzuno.

"Oh, great, yet more of her...
.................oh."

Remembering that he was still on duty, he put the phone back, closed the locker, and tackled the bookkeeping.

"...........I put the nine o'clock sales journal into the books, Ms. Kisaki."

"Hmm? Oh, thanks."

He made for the door, half jogging back to work. Kawata stopped him on the way.

"Hey, something up, Marko? You don't look good."

Maou marveled at this. He hadn't noticed anything—but did the color really drain from his face *that* quickly?

"No, um…"

What could Suzuno be thinking? After all that nonsense she planted in Acieth's mind, *that* was what she wanted him to see? It'd be yet another disaster by the time Acieth woke up, no doubt.

"I'm just…really not looking forward to going home today…"

"Huh?!"

"I wish I could spend the night somewhere else, even…"

"Wow, you're starting to freak me out. Did something hit you on the head, or what? You can go home early if you want; I can close for ya. You got your roommates and that kimono chick waiting, don'tcha?"

Kawata was always a bit blunt like that. But the reaction to his half-jealous, half-teasing offer was nothing short of dramatic.

"Oh, man, I got someone *far* worse'n that waiting for me! I don't wanna go home, I don't wanna go home, I don't wanna go home! I'm gonna have *such* a pain in the ass waiting for me! I just wanna keep my head down and do my work, and people bring all this stupid shit over for me, god*dammit*, take care of your *own* dumb shit for a change!!"

"M-Marko?!"

"And like *you're* one to talk, Suzuno! What the hell was up with that text?! I *just* told you to stop acting out of line like that!"

He ran off, exhibiting his full, unbridled emotions for a change.

"Did I say something bad?" the dumbfounded Kawata asked himself.

But perhaps Maou couldn't be blamed for this outburst. Here was the full content of the text that Suzuno sent him:

"Go home immediately after work. ❤ Emilia is waiting. ❤"

"I don't wanna go *hoooooooooooooooooooome…*"

It was half past midnight, the MgRonald doors firmly closed behind him, and Maou was walking the Dullahan II back home. Suzuno's text had distracted him so thoroughly from his work that he had made several careless errors. His heart just wasn't in it. He looked at the text one more time, sighed, and stopped.

"Wait… They weren't gonna wait up all night for me, were they?"

Even if he was willing to let the heart emojis slide as just another sign of Suzuno's conflicting lifestyle, what did she mean by, "Emilia is waiting"? Judging by the Hero's act over on Shinjuku-sanchome, she couldn't be in any shape to reason over matters with Laila or Amane. He had assumed she went back home, to Eifukucho, with Emeralda.

Chiho waiting up for him would make a little sense, at least. Really, Chiho's home wasn't safe. She lived with her parents, which meant that she ought to be back there in terms of social norms or whatnot, but she was no Hero or sorceress. She had nothing to defend herself with, and leaving the apartment to return home would be, under the circumstances, a fairly courageous choice. And even if she had Amane's or Shiba's support, there was an inherent time lag involved—something Amane proved just this evening. Along those lines, convincing Chiho's parents to let her remain someplace within sight of Maou, Suzuno, or Shiba would make sense.

But no. It was *Emi* waiting for him. Why was Emi—a woman whom everyone believed could be shot from behind with a tank round and not even get a bruise—waiting at Maou's apartment for him? And if Suzuno chose that moment to text him about it, who was she with right now? Nord, or Ashiya? One of the two.

"Oh, man, it'd suck if they were in the middle of some huge argument when I get back. Uggh…"

He ignored her in Urushihara's hospital room and took great pains to avoid contact after that, so Maou still didn't know where Laila lived. But if Emi and Laila were to have a family squabble under the roof of Villa Rosa Sasazuka, the very future of Japan would be called into question.

"Probably not, though. It's too quiet tonight for that."

Still standing there on the sidewalk, he put Dullahan II's kickstand down and looked behind him.

"So are you gonna help me procrastinate on getting home, or...?"

"Ooh, you saw me?"

"What made you think I wouldn't?"

There he found the archangel Gabriel, in his customary toga and T-shirt. Between his size and the general distaste Maou had for him, there was no way he'd ever fail to notice him in an otherwise empty street.

"Mikitty sent me here, all right? Y'know how Emilia got attacked. She wanted to be sure nobody at the apartment was goin' around alone."

"I don't need a bodyguard," Maou snapped.

"Yeah, I bet Emilia didn't think so, either. And look what *that* got ya!"

"Either way, I don't want *you* as a bodyguard."

"Aw, don't be such a meanie! I'm just a loyal knight in service, mm-kay?"

"Knight to *whom*?"

"Oh, and don't worry about Chiho Sasaki, either. I walked her home and put a full alert network around her house, so if something comes up, we'll take care of it."

"I didn't ask you about her, and the idea of you walking her home and doing *anything* around her house freaks me the hell out."

"Aw, why are you being so suspicious? I'm an angel!"

"You don't remember what Chiho said the first time she saw you?"

"Ah-ha-ha!"

Maou sat down on the ground, the fatigue seeping into the core of his being.

"What? Did work take a lot out of ya?"

"Yeah, and you just struck the final blow... Look, is Emi really waiting for me back home?"

"Huh? Ohh, well, I *did* see the girl. Chiho Sasaki went home around ten PM, but I think the other one was still there. Dunno about now, but..."

"I sure wish she'd go away... I don't wanna get caught in all that pent-up rage she's got for her mom..."

"Yeah, well, there's only one home for you to return to! Arise, Lord of All Demons! One foot in front of the other! And chin up! Alciel's dinner awaits!"

"Aaaaaaaahhhh, why can't someone come through my door and give me a life where I can just shut up and focus on my work? This is driving me *craaaaaazy*!!"

The sheer insane tension in Gabriel's voice was the last thing Maou wanted to hear. He just wanted to curl up and cry on the spot. But he knew it wouldn't do anything good for him, so he pushed his bicycle onward, Gabriel joining him by his side.

"Hey, hey, can I ask you something?"

"What?" Maou replied, not bothering to lift his head up.

"Why won't you just hear Laila out?"

"No reason to."

"Why not?"

"I dunno. If you're hoping for some long-winded answer, sorry. I really just got no reason to, that's all."

There was little in the way of emotion to Maou's voice.

"I mean, I appreciate her saving my life, long ago. I do, but I've been dancing in the palm of her hand long enough. Plus, I just saved *her* life today. I paid her back everything I owed, with interest."

"Mm-hmm, mm-hmm. All right, I get it. I get it, but, hmm, I guess I also don't get it? You've been so flexible dealing with all the trouble that's come your way in Japan. It's not like you to completely turn Laila down like that. Don'tcha think you're missing out on something?"

"Like what?"

"Like, you know Laila's in pretty deep with the Yesod children, right? You don't think hearing her out could help with, y'know, stuff going forward?"

"...Have you ever raised a kid, Gabriel?"

"Hmm?"

Gabriel blinked at the sideswipe.

"When I started raising Alas Ramus, I seriously considered getting some insurance."

"Insurance? You mean, like, life or fire insurance, that kind of thing?" Gabriel seriously pondered this for a moment, even though the context suggested Maou never bought any. "Is the demon realm worried about long-term risk management nowadays?"

"I didn't do it in the end. The premiums are ridiculous, I had to get a full physical, and there was a lot of other dumb crap. But you know why I thought about it? Because I realized, however unlikely it was, there was absolutely a chance that I'd get killed, and it'd be *your* fault."

"Oh, *my* fault!" Gabriel clapped his hands as it dawned on him. He *did* have the Devil King's death in the works, once, back when he wasn't quite so shy about throwing his powers around.

"But more generally speaking... You know, I had no idea how things were gonna turn out, so I thought I should join up in case something happened."

"Yeah, I hear you there."

The lights from Villa Rosa Sasazuka were now visible in the distance.

"On the other hand, if everyone *did* know the future, it'd be impossible to make money selling insurance."

"Riiiight..."

"And I don't want to know what's waiting in Alas Ramus's future."

"Ooh, you think that's a good idea? As her guardian? If you got a hunch something bad's coming up, shouldn't you be aware of that?"

"Well," Maou sharply rebuked, "what if that bad thing I 'got a hunch' about can't be avoided, no matter what? You weren't around for it, but my landlord told me that Alas Ramus and Acieth need to go back to the heavens. *She* told me that. And *she's* been connected to Laila since who knows when. So if I 'hear her out,' as you put it, it means I'm gonna have to send Alas Ramus and Acieth away. To heaven. Something neither Emi nor I intend to do. I don't want

Alas Ramus goin' somewhere that far away from me, and she doesn't want to leave us, either. So everything's fine. Just the way it is."

"...Not that I'm one to talk, but 'what you don't know won't hurt you' ain't true all the time, y'know?"

"No, you're *not* one to talk about that. And I'd advise you to be careful. She's sleeping now, but Acieth's always going on about how she wants to kill you whenever she sees you. There's no tellin' when she might strike atcha in bed when the landlord's not paying attention."

"Yeah, ahh, she's tried a few times already, soooooo..."

"Too bad you didn't let her finish the job."

"Oh, you are being *such* a meanie tonight!"

They kept walking as they bickered, until they finally reached Villa Rosa Sasazuka just before one in the morning. Parking the Dullahan II, Maou turned back toward Gabriel.

"Thanks for guarding me. You're relieved of duty."

"Oh, at least let me hear the story to the end, mm-kay? I'm curious!"

"What do you mean, 'to the end'...?" Maou rolled his eyes. "...See, that's exactly what drives me up the wall the most."

"Hmm?"

"You're right. I can't avoid everything just because I keep myself in the dark about it. So, yeah, maybe I *should* make an effort to know what you guys and Laila have been up to. But you know what?" Maou pointed at his own chest. "Why," he softly spoke, "do we have to expend all our strength every time we find out about something? Since when did we agree to take that on?"

"Even if it winds up destroying worlds?"

"I don't care."

"It could wipe out any future your descendants could ever have, mm-kay?"

"If you mean humans are gonna die out, then great. I'm a demon. And if you mean demons, I'm gonna be dead by then anyway. Let *them* figure something out."

"But you all have strength. The kind of strength nobody else has, you know? That could help solve all of this, but you still aren't gonna move on it?"

The Lord of All Demons smiled as he shut his eyes tightly in a wince.

"...So *that's* how you really feel?"

"Huh?"

"Well, lemme turn that around on you. Why should I let people push all this responsibility on me just because I've got strength?"

"Oh? ...Ohhhhh."

Gabriel ran out of words for a moment, unable to counter Maou's logic.

"You guys just wanna do it all over again, don't you? Like, 'O the Hero Emilia, thou art the only one with the power to smite the evil Devil King Satan. Venture forth, and bring us his head!'"

The smile disappeared.

"And what'll that get Emi? Huh?"

"Um..."

"I mean, I can think of several motives why Emi might be after my life. I know what I did to her, and I know she wants to follow through on her anger and earn that release for herself. But all the humans on Ente Isla joined the bandwagon on that, didn't they? They took the burden they all should've borne equally and just plopped it all on her. Just because she was strong."

This was the sin committed by the entire human population of Ente Isla—something Emeralda regretted to this day. It led to her imprisonment in Efzahan, locking her heart there as surely as if behind iron bars.

"She chased me right into a corner, let me go, kept on chasing, and just when she almost had me, her closest confidant betrayed her. And until Emeralda, Albert, Suzuno, and I did something about it, you had every human over there dancing in heaven's hand. Why do I have to save *their* future? Do I have any reason at all to do that?"

"...So you don't want to because Ente Islans are a bunch of sinners?"

"No, you still don't get it." Maou gave Gabriel a withering sneer. "Me and Emi are doing just fine here. It's, like, super chill. So why do we have to throw all that away and take on a piece of your moldy old plan yet again? Like, is that a joke, or what?"

"Aw, whaaa—? *That's* kinda selfish."

"*Who's* selfish?" Maou spat out. "Lemme ask you: Do rich people have a duty to throw all their money at the world's poor until they're bankrupt?"

"Um…"

"Do you think poor people should just unhinge their mouths like baby birds and wait for someone to give 'em worms?"

Gabriel fell silent.

"If me and Emi are more powerful than anyone else, do we have a duty to abandon everything in our lives to help the world out? Hmm? Who put that kind of duty upon us?"

The anger and irritation were now clearly present in his voice.

"That's exactly what I hate about dealing with you guys. Like, 'Ooh, you've got the power, you'll do it for us!' You approach us like that because you assume we're always gonna be like 'Oh, sure, we've got a responsibility to work hard for you all, let's do it.'"

"N-not to thaaaat extent… Hey, it's the middle of the night, try to keep it down a bit…"

"It's not? So what's your motive, then? Tell me."

"I-I'm not gonna defend myself, but *Laila's* not like that at *all*, mm-kay? She's risked her life up to now, trying to keep all this destruction at bay. She wants to keep Emilia and Nord safe, and she just wants the world of Ente Isla to get back to the *right* direction, as much as she can…"

It was rare for Gabriel to step up to defend someone else. Maou easily brushed it aside.

"Aha… I see. And that's the attitude you all are taking? Great. *Now* I get it. I should've known. You're the kind of dude who figures that a couple scratches aren't gonna break a steel plate, huh?"

"Um? S-steel?"

The sudden gear change bewildered Gabriel.

"Steel's really strong, right? It's not gonna break if just any old thing hits it, and it'll stay sturdy no matter how much it's damaged. Right?"

"R-right..."

"Does that make it okay to hit it?"

"Huh?"

"I *said*, if you can't *hurt* it, does that make it okay to *hit it*?!"

He was now shouting. A far-off dog howled at the sound.

"If it's that sturdy, does that make it okay to punch it, kick it, throw it around? If it's hard to damage it, does that mean it's all right to treat it like garbage? If it's strong enough to deal with it, does that mean it doesn't care *how* you use and abuse it? If me, and Emi, and Ashiya and Urushihara and Suzuno all do the dance you're tellin' us to, are you gonna guarantee that we'll have a life to go back to afterward?! Or are all our lives expendable enough compared to the world or mankind?"

"...Um. Yeah. I—I see what you mean." Gabriel nodded, finally beginning to follow Maou's fervent argument. "And I say that because you convinced me, mm-kay?"

"...You really understand now?"

"Oh, you bet. It's kind of like, y'know, someone's griping atcha about the environment and saving our precious nature, and you visit their house and they got all the lights on and the AC cranked up to max. It's like, who the hell they think are, huh?"

"...If *that's* the example you bring up, I'd say you're just as infected by life here as we are."

For the first time that night, Maou softened his expression.

"But...yeah. I guess Laila wants us to do something, but for us, there's no reason, no responsibility, no duty, no merit, no *nothing* to hear her out. Ente Isla's politically stable, the demon realm is chilling out, and heaven's cut itself off from Earth. To me, the only outstanding issues are taking care of that guy who gave Chi and Emi a scare tonight, and...well, how I oughtta square up my relationship with Emi, I guess. And once that's all done, we'll both live however way we want to. And I'm *not* gonna let you guys interfere with that."

"There's a *lot* I could say about that..." Gabriel grinned. "But if you wanna live however way you want to, does that mean trying to conquer Ente Isla again, or...? 'Cause we might try to stop you."

"And that's fine. Go right ahead. I'm not expecting zero resistance, and I'm ready to eliminate anything in my way. What I'm *not* ready to do is go out on this playing field I know nothing about, being controlled by the puppet strings of good faith. You said I've dealt with a lot of trouble here on Earth, but if I didn't, it would've put either myself or someone close to me in danger. I never once did any of that for the sake of the world or whatever."

"I see, I see. You had the strength and force of will to unite the demon realm at such a relatively young age. You care for your companions. And now I see Laila completely misunderstood all of that. If you're puttin' it that way, I doubt she's gonna get her say with you for a few hundred years."

"Glad I made myself understood. I'm going home. You do that, too."

"Yeah, guess I oughtta."

They were under the apartment's stairway when they went their separate ways.

"Y'know, though," Gabriel called from below once Maou was fully up the stairs, "it might've been a mistake for you to bring up that topic with me."

"What?"

He flashed a proud smile at the dubious Maou.

"Hey, I'm just sayin', I've gotten on in my life a bit more than you."

"Yeah, right. I dunno how you and Laila are connected behind the scenes, but I wanna hear from you even less than I do from her."

"Right, right, right. Let's leave it at that for now, yeah? 'Night."

"Yeah."

"Also..."

"Hmm?"

"Careful on your way back home."

"Huh?"

"I dunno if you were paying attention or not, but, ah, don't write checks with your mouth you can't cash with your butt, mm-kay?"

With that apparently meaningful advice, Gabriel set off into the cold night, sandals pattering over to Shiba's place next door. It was odd. Once the stairwell gate was open, it was just a short distance to Room 201. What was there to be careful about...?

"Oh, damn, it's one AM. Bet they're probably asleep by now."

Maou winced as he opened the gate. All that time wasted in conversation with Gabriel.

"Whoa!"

Then he almost whooped in surprise as he took a step back.

"Wh-what the hell?! You *still* haven't gone away?!"

Emi was standing there.

The glare from the half–burned out tube light running along the walkway behind her made it hard to gauge her expression, but she was still wearing the same clothes from Shinjuku-sanchome. She must have never gone home. There was no light from either Room 201 or 202—his roommates and Suzuno must all have retired. Maou expected Emi might be staying with Suzuno tonight. But why was she standing here on this sleepy walkway like some possessive spirit while everyone else was gone?

"Um...did I wake you? S-sorry."

The apology came softly. He was shouting at Gabriel downstairs. Perhaps Emi was nodding off just then, coming to give him a piece of her mind once he was done.

"But I mean, you know what you and Chi ran into today. And then my landlord decided to send Gabriel to guard me, which I *really* don't appreciate. All the crap he was giving me, I couldn't help but get a little loud with him, so... Like, seriously? An archangel body-guard for the Devil King? Ha-ha-ha-ha-ha.................. Emi?"

There was no reaction to any of that. Maou began to feel a tad creeped out.

"Emi? Um, wh-what's up? Hellooooo?"

He tried waving his hand a little.

"...You're late. Alas Ramus finally fell asleep just now. She was waiting for you."

"O-oh? B-but you knew, didn't you? I was clo—"

Closing tonight is what he never managed to blurt out. He felt a slight breeze. Then, the next thing he knew, Maou was being embraced by Emi.

"Hnn?!?!"

She's gonna kill me!

It was the only conclusion to make. He didn't know what riled Emi up so badly. She must've really hated being woken up. Feeling Emi's arms behind his neck, Maou froze, already picturing them twisting his vertebrae in terrifying directions. He'd never have enough time to harness the demonic force in Room 201's closet. Up to this point, between their duel on Ente Isla and this encounter on his doorstop, Emi had mercilessly attacked Maou on more than one or two occasions. Never, though, had she exercised her force in such a brutal, primitive way.

This is it.

But as he stood there, tensed up and preparing for the worst, he discovered that the fateful moment didn't seem to be arriving.

"...Oh?"

Realizing he was still alive, five seconds later, Maou opened the eyes he had reflexively shut tight.

"......"

"Ummmm...?"

He could see Emi's head right below his line of sight. Her weight leaned against his shoulders and neck a little. Her face was against his chest. What did this mean? Perhaps it wasn't a neck-breaker finishing hold, executed the moment they met—but if it wasn't, then Maou had no idea what it was.

"It's fine."

"Huh?"

He heard the voice from around his chest, more clearly than he expected.

"It's fine."

The sentence only confused Maou further the second time he heard it. He didn't know *what* was "fine," exactly, but he detected no anger in her voice, so he understood that Emi wasn't mad at him, at least.

He knew that, but as his mind cooled down and he impartially analyzed how he should view this, he could feel his blood pressure start to fall. No matter how you looked at this, anyone would interpret it to be Suzuno and Rika's ridiculous ravings come to life. To Maou, the term *paired together*—distilled by Acieth from their MgRonald conversation—didn't mean anything apart from physical contact. *Physical contact*, however, was the only way to describe this.

It made Maou realize that the only way out of this was to keep his cool. Getting agitated, in his mind or in his soul, could easily alarm Acieth. She didn't need telepathy or an Idea Link for it; her fusion with him made it unavoidable. But if Acieth woke up right now, the way people would look at him tomorrow would be horrifying. It'd be worse than waking up in a parallel world, a whole other dimension of space.

"I..."

"Uh, yeah?"

He had no idea what she was thinking. But Emi's voice was calm, composed. He knew she had a reason for this. It was best, he thought, to avoid prodding her too much, lest he make things worse. So he stayed frozen, figuring that listening to Emi was the most practical solution at hand.

"I never thought that I wanted someone to help me before. By the time I was grown up, I could take care of pretty much anything by myself."

"O-oh, yeah? Well, you're the strongest Hero the human race ever had."

"And Eme, and Al, and even Olba way back when, they'd help me out when needed, without me having to say anything. We kinda knew what each of us was thinking, always. So even if setting off to kill you was tough, sometimes, I never thought about quitting. Not once."

"......Really? Well, great."

It was clearly not the right thing to say, but Maou nodded anyway.

"But back there, in Efzahan..."

"Oh, yeah, back there."

He could only humor her, utterly lost as to where this was going. It made what came next even more powerful.

"I felt, for the first time...*protected*."

"...Ah?"

Maou had two reasons for that questioning grunt of his. One, he simply didn't understand the meaning of it. Two, Emi's body had started to shake a little.

"...Why you?"

"Wh-what...?"

"Why did you protect me, after making such a complete mess of my life...?"

"..."

I'm not the only one protecting you, lady.

Maou thought it. But not even he was oblivious enough to say it. Emi was, in a word, venting. Emi hadn't forgotten about the friendship and sacrifices Emeralda, Albert, Chiho, Rika, and Suzuno made for her. But her mind was exhausted, to the point that not even those memories could support her. The events in Efzahan had already damaged her enough—Laila's appearance shook her even worse. It was best just to let her say whatever she wanted. To let it all out. And as far as Maou was concerned, he didn't mind playing the punching bag if it meant he made it out alive.

"My father used to protect me all the time."

"Uh-huh."

"But that ended, thanks to you."

"I'm not gonna make any excuses for that."

"And after that, it was me who had to keep protecting people. Since...I was the strongest of them."

"Right."

"And I'm still stronger than anyone...so..." Emi's shoulders twitched. "My father won't protect me anymore."

"..."

Maou could tell: In that statement was embedded a lifetime's worth of dark memories. She had reunited with Nord, tasked with keeping him safe—but she still believed his presence would provide an emotional support for her. But in that hospital room, her father stepped up to protect her mother instead. Faced with the overwhelming strength of the daughter he once risked his life to save, Nord decided to risk it all not for Emi's heart, but for his wife's body. The moment Laila appeared there, there was no chance the family would ever rebuild itself peacefully.

"It's just you."

"Huh?"

"Right now, when I'm stronger than anybody else, only you protected me. Only you. The man who I thought ruined my life."

"...Um, are you sure you're thinking straight?"

"I am. And I'm not drunk, either."

"I'd hope not. You're underage."

"No, I'm not. My ID lists me as twenty. The Japanese police don't have anything on me."

"Not a very Hero-like thing to say."

"I'm not any kind of hero. It's just that people keep calling me that. That career doesn't even exist in this world."

Now he could feel her smiling as she quivered. Smiling, while shedding tears. She held him a notch more tightly.

"Talk about the devil tempting me. You were the only one who gave me the words I wanted to hear. Even just now..."

Maou could feel his blood stiffen once more. Did Gabriel say all that because he knew Emi was here? There might have been no helping it, but Maou's words did imply on multiple occasions that he saw Emi and Suzuno as "his" people. People he needed to protect.

"Uh, how much did you hear?" he asked, his voice hoarse.

"I was waiting for you all night," she replied, chidingly. "With Alas Ramus. I could hear everything once you were here."

"…This is awful," he said, grinning as he repeated Gabriel's conversation in his mind. "Could this even *get* any more awkward? Shit. This has to be some evil god screwing with me."

"But isn't it about time I have the right to live just for myself? I think so, but there's something in my mind that tells me I can't. I know Eme and Bell respect my wishes. Chiho does, too. But I can't drive away that sense of pride I have—the idea that I need to use my powers to help my friends. It's not that I don't want to help keep Chiho and everybody safe. But when it's all said and done, I can't solve anything by myself. Why do people keep calling me the Hero? All this strength, and I can't even keep myself intact, much less my friends. And now Laila, of all people, is helping me. I can't carry any more of this burden. I can't…!"

Her voice began to shake, her body expressing both her tears and her tormented heart. Maou didn't respond by hugging her tighter. He just let it unfold. She was venting. Shoving cold reason in her face right now wouldn't help anyone.

"There's just nothing I can do, and people still call me a hero. They ask me to keep fighting, to keep throwing my strength around… I can't even save myself; what else do these people want…?"

"Well, I want you to wrap up your training period already, so you can join the crew full-time."

"…" Emi's sobbing stopped. The statement caught her off guard. "…You never change, do you? I'm starting not to hate it so much."

"Hey, if something's on my mind, I say it."

"But you're always hiding something, too."

"I don't see why I have to show the entire world what kinda hand I'm playin' with." Maou sighed, and—for the first time—reached out to touch Emi's shoulders. "Lemme be frank with you. I didn't say all that stuff because I wanted to curry favor with you, you got that?"

"I know. That… That's why I'm happy about it."

"Huhh?"

"You meant everything you said, and that feels great. Maybe you won't admit it, but as mean as you've been to me in the past, you've always protected me as a friend... Well, no, more like a neighbor."

"Well, yeah, because I had to..."

"Whether you had to or not, there aren't many people who can protect someone like me."

"...Man, you're a hot mess tonight."

"Of course I am. Why would I be saying all this to the Devil King otherwise?"

Emi removed her face from Maou's chest, her tearful face smiling as she looked at him. The corners of her eyes were red and irritated.

"Thank you, Devil King. I'm built pretty tough, so a little maintenance work and I'll be right back to normal."

"Is that why you've been acting so weird lately? People used 'n' abused you so much that your brain crashed?"

"Yeah. It crashed hard today. I'm just not normal right now."

She sighed softly, then took a step back from Maou.

"...Emi?"

She still held him by the hand. "Can I ask you a question?"

"What?"

"If... If I keep getting weaker like this...will you protect me?"

"Whoa, dang, I think your brain's still crashing on you. What are you talking about?"

"I told you," Emi replied as her face reddened, "I'm not normal yet."

Looking down at the hand clasped around the young woman's, Maou's watch told him it was almost half past one.

"Well, look, no matter how much the world changes, the truth never does, right?"

"Huh?"

"You, the proud Hero, were there, too, right?"

"...Oh."

Emi knew what Maou was referring to. That day in Sasazuka when they all came together, and Chiho found out the truth about Ente Isla.

"I never really saw it that way, but if I'm 'protecting' you, it's just 'cause I'm lending you a hand since you're so incapable of doing it yourself. With all that strength, no less. If you were weak, I wouldn't even bother."

"...Nice thing to say to someone whose brain was just fried."

"I don't care if you're weak, or getting weaker," Maou casually countered. "But I hate people who try to make their weakness a weapon. What I want from you is the girl who goes around bragging about how she's the Hero and struggling hard for the sake of her friends. Everyone has a brain freeze sometimes, but there's no room in the Devil King's Army for habitual whiners. The title of Great Demon General is given only to people with superior hearts, minds, and bodies."

"...Is it?" Emi nodded slightly, making something up in her mind, and finally removed her grasp on Maou's hand. "Well, mind and body's one thing, but I'm kind of annoyed at the idea that I lose out to Lucifer heart-wise."

"Wow. Low blow."

"Am I wrong?"

"Though I have to admit, all the Great Demon General stuff aside, you'd need to work pretty damn hard to be worse than Urushihara at keeping your act together."

Emi gave a chuckle to that thought. It struck Maou as odd.

"I guess you're always gonna be my archenemy after all, huh? I knew I shouldn't have expected any kind words from you."

"You definitely shouldn't," he replied. "In fact, it's dumb to even utter it. But even if you weren't my nemesis, you sure aren't livin' up to your good name right now."

"No. I guess not. I don't think so, either. It's just...crazy how bad this day's turned out."

"You're only human. I know things were discouraging for you. But at least try to make sure your actions don't get misunderstood. You know how sensitive the people around you are to that."

"Oh?" Emi smiled, her face still reddened. "I wonder what they'd think if they saw us embracing each other?"

"Don't embellish it. It wasn't 'each other.' You plowed into me the moment I saw you."

"You don't have to phrase it like a car accident."

"It was one of the most harrowing experiences of my life."

Maou sincerely meant it. Oddly, the woman didn't seem to mind.

"That hurts, you know."

"Not as much as it hurt *me*, man. I'm going to bed. I got work tomorrow."

He walked past Emi, down the walkway, and put his hand on Room 201's door.

"All right. Thanks. Sorry to bother you this late."

"...Sure," he said, not turning around as he unlocked the door. He shut it behind him, never giving Emi another glance.

Moonlight was the only illumination inside. Ashiya was sleeping on the tatami-mat floor, as was Urushihara, unfairly robbed of the closet space he called home. Considering the Hero was lying in ambush for the Devil King's return all evening, it demonstrated a worrisome lack of security. The rice cooker was turned off, and on the table were three balls of seasoned rice, covered in plastic wrap. They were all irregularly shaped, not the neat little balls Maou was used to seeing.

"What the hell...?" His voice was soft, whispering, so that Emi (presumably next door) wouldn't hear him. "These look ridiculous," he muttered, snorting as he grabbed up one of the misshapen blobs.

THE DEVIL
AND THE HERO
ARE GIVEN A
PROPOSITION

"Ladies and gentlemen! The day is here!"

At Mayumi Kisaki's order, her staff stiffened their posture.

"It hasn't been easy going, but as of today, the Hatagaya station MgRonald is officially part of our company's delivery program!"

The gauntlet was thrown. Beginning ten AM today, deliveries from Hatagaya station were all systems go. The franchise had been allotted three Gyro-Roofs, the three-wheeled motorcycles commonly used for small-scale local deliveries. Their bodies shone a bright shade of red, the MgRonald logo brilliantly emblazoned upon them.

"It's a great honor to have you guys on our first-ever delivery shift. Remember what you learned in training and give this job everything you've got."

""Yes, ma'am!"" the entire morning crew shouted in unison.

Maou and Kawata had been selected as delivery drivers for the first day. Emi would mainly handle order-taking duties on the phone, while Kisaki was the utility person, ready to tackle whatever was needed—for example, hopping on a scooter to cover for orders that came when Maou and Kawata were busy with previous ones. All this, of course, done alongside their usual duties when no delivery orders were waiting.

This being the first day, Maou and Kawata were understandably nervous. The Hatagaya station location wasn't just handling standard MgRonald deliveries; it was part of an experimental test program, and thus they were expecting more delivery orders than other locations.

No one had noticed since Kisaki had Emi set up to be the phone operator from the very beginning, but other MgRonalds usually didn't take phone orders. Instead, customers used their computers or smartphones to look up local restaurants and make their orders online. Kisaki, however, didn't feel that was enough. Her take on it, as loudly given to the area manager: Given her store's location in the middle of a busy neighborhood and shopping area, it would be silly for them not to take direct phone orders. No matter how common smartphones had become, some people would always prefer to do things the old-fashioned way, and restricting deliveries to Internet orders only, in Kisaki's mind, would be needlessly driving away potential business.

"Noodle places, Chinese restaurants, pizza joints, and sushi restaurants have been offering phone delivery for decades," she explained. "With the Net, you have to sign up for an account and every site has a different system. Compared to that, calling in orders is stupid easy. Just say what you want, and *bam*. This idea that young people will use nothing but the Internet for everything is a fantasy peddled by people who don't use their brains. Customers, young or old, will use whatever's easiest for them at that moment. Especially in the next few decades, when Japan's population will get older and older, it'll be key to target exactly the kind of group who's *not* used to doing things online. Everything's gonna be on the Net sooner or later, but we need to keep a focus on people who are fine with the old system, or else we're shooting ourselves in the foot."

This was all very familiar to Emi. During her stint as a call-center operator for Dokodemo, she noticed that questions from middle-aged and elderly customers took up a significant chunk of her workload. Having a chance to bring those skills to MgRonald—especially considering she thought the audience for fast-food burgers would skew younger than that—would be a plus for her, experience-wise.

"Don't forget, of course, that your nondelivery duties remain as important as ever. I'll be expecting all of you to maintain the same high level of performance you've shown me before. Dismissed!"

With their marching papers handed to them, the crew set out to prepare for morning traffic.

"Talk about déjà vu, huh?"

As she put on her headset and adjusted the mic position to her liking, Emi couldn't help but feel a bit excited. Starting today, everyone on the staff—whether working the café, kitchen, or dining hall—would be wearing these headsets for a time. With a larger head count and much more varied array of operations to deal with, Kisaki brought them in to help streamline things and keep everyone on the same page. Whenever the mic entered her view, Emi felt more sharply than ever that she was working just that much harder.

Her role was unique in that it could accept phone calls. Customer information like addresses and phone numbers needed to be typed into a computer for deliveries, and Kisaki figured that doing this while trying to cradle a phone receiver between your head and shoulder was inefficient and detrimental to good customer service. The headset would also be indispensable for communicating with drivers—the bikes didn't have GPS devices, and not everyone on staff necessarily had the local roads memorized, so Emi would need to provide directions in case drivers got lost. (They could use the GPS on their phones, of course, but not everybody had a smartphone.)

There was talk of hiring on a permanent employee or two to exclusively handle deliveries, depending on how busy they found themselves. However, given that everyone on staff needed at least a passing familiarity with how MgRonald worked and Kisaki wanted to retain a small group of experts who could handle any on-site duty needed, it was likely the entire crew would eventually get rotated in and out of delivery work.

"Saemi, can you hear me?"

"…Um, yes!" came the slightly delayed response from Emi. She wasn't quite used to Kisaki calling her that yet.

"Given your performance during training, I'm positive you're the right staffer for this position. You're gonna be our eyes in the delivery control tower from the first day. Do your best."

"Got it. I'll try to live up to expectations."

"Thanks."

Emi smiled at Kisaki, who was at the other end of the kitchen. The manager smiled back and gave her a thumbs-up.

❋

Whenever a staff member wrapped up their probationary period, there was a little ceremony that the crew came to call The Holy Christening. It was the moment when Kisaki began calling you by her personally selected nickname, and for Emi, the day came immediately after that fateful late night she spent exposing her anxieties to Maou. She had no regrets about it, oddly enough—when morning came, she felt supremely refreshed.

Strolling in for her shift just before lunch, she breezed past the grimacing Maou and changed into her MgRonald uniform, which she was finally starting to get used to. The moment she went back into the dining hall:

"Morning, Saemi!"

"Um, good…morning…"

It came so suddenly, Kisaki just cutting across her path and whizzing on by, that Emi's expression was classic deer-in-the-headlights.

"Oh, are you out of training, Yusa?"

"Huh?"

The question was lobbed by Akiko Ohki (or "Aki-chan" around the kitchen), a veteran crewmember with a history as long as Maou's and Kawata's.

"Ms. Kisaki just called you by a nickname, didn't she?"

"Oh, was that a, uh, nickname?"

"Mm-hmm," Akiko said with a bemused grin. "Everybody makes

that face the first time they hear it. It always comes out of nowhere, so I was pretty surprised with mine, too."

"Ah...ha..." Emi replied, still unsure what all this meant as Kawata approached them.

"At this MgRonald," he explained, "it's kind of an unwritten rule that if Ms. Kisaki starts using a nickname, you're officially a full-fledged part of the team. What'd she call you?"

"Uhmm..." It came so suddenly that she couldn't immediately recall. "I think it was 'Saemi'..."

"Oooh!" Akiko beamed. "That's not a common pattern."

"Yeah, but your full name's only four syllables, Yusa, so that probably felt more natural to her then trying to add extra sounds to it."

The sight of these coworkers getting excited about dumb nicknames perplexed Emi. Then she noticed another, much larger, change:

"Hey, Saemi, we're short on oolong-tea concentrate today, so make sure that doesn't get red-lighted during the peak, okay?"

"Saemi, do a cleaning run on number ten for me."

"Oh, Saemi, you put the tray paper on upside down a couple times today. It's an easy mistake to make when you're busy, so keep an eye out for that."

Kisaki was speaking completely differently to her. She went out of her way to call her things like "Ms. Yusa" before, always couching her requests and orders in polite terms. Now she barked at her just as she did with Maou or Chiho. It didn't mean Kisaki was refusing to help or turning up the pressure on her, but it *was* subtly different.

"Well," Akiko said when Emi asked about it, "this is just a guess, but there are a lot of crappy jobs in the restaurant business, you know? And people sometimes quit during their training period, so maybe she's politer then so she doesn't leave a bad impression if they do. If it doesn't work out, she wouldn't want it to be because she acted like a slave driver, you know?"

Kawata nodded his approval. "Yeah, come to think of it, that's how she was with me at first, too."

Akiko gave this a cheerful laugh. "Either way," she reflected, "I think that's the fastest hiring-to-nickname time since Chi. You're probably gonna see a pretty big bump in your hourly wage, too. Hee-hee! Guess I got some competition now."

This mainly served to make Emi awkwardly stiffen her posture.

✳

Between that day and today, about half of the employees had taken to calling Emilia "Saemi." Chiho and Kawata stuck with "Yusa," since they were used to it by now.

Maou, meanwhile, stuck with just "Emi."

"Hey, can someone go downstairs and check to see if we've got extra maintenance brushes? The one up here's getting too threadbare to use."

"I'll go look now. If I find one, I'll bring it up."

"Oh, um, thanks, Emi."

Emi reflexively smiled at the mixed feelings she heard through the headset.

His attitude toward Emi on the job was no longer very different from what it was off duty. Emi, meanwhile, was making a concerted effort to continue treating him as the veteran employee he was. He had the most experience out of anyone on the team, and she was still the new girl. Giving Maou her usual amount of lip would no doubt raise eyebrows—and while Maou didn't bring it up, perhaps understanding what her thoughts were, something still seemed to bother him about it.

It was odd, though. When she first signed on, playing the "student" role to Maou's "teacher" took a somewhat concerted acting effort much of the time. It also made Maou act all high and mighty around her, which was even more irritating. Since that night, though, she felt interacting with him came far more naturally now. She didn't need to constantly think about her position in the MgRonald hierarchy any longer.

"Hee-hee-hee-hee-hee..."

"Wh-what's so funny, Aki-chan?"

The evil cackling from Akiko as she watched Emi scurry down to the basement surprised Kawata a little.

"Oh, it's just... You know, Saemi's gotten used to things pretty well now, huh? And meanwhile, Maou's acting so awkward around her. I thought it was kinda funny."

"Ahh... Yeah, I don't get those two sometimes. It does feel like Yusa's been loosening up lately, but..."

In Kawata's mind, Emi had been shouldering some heavy burden until a few days ago. That atmosphere was now a thing of the past.

"But they were all friends, right? Maou and Chi and Saemi? Oh, and have you looked at Chi lately, Kawatchi? She's hilarious."

"You're thinking something highly nefarious, aren't you, Aki-chan?"

"No pulling the wool over your eyes, huh? Well, whenever Maou and Saemi are talking lately, Chi makes this incredibly goofy face."

"Goofy? Goofy how?"

"I mean, it starts with this really warm smile, like a mom looking at her kids. Then her eyebrows go down, like she's a scientist working through a tough question or something. And then all the color drains from her face, like she's seen a ghost."

"Ahh..." Kawata gave a broad nod to this as he stared off into the distance. "One day, on a moonless night, someone needs to stab Maou in the back."

"Oh, yeah, totally! You know what I'm talking about?"

"*Aki-chan, Kawatchi, what's going on? You aren't working.*"

Kisaki's headset interruption quickly spurred them back into action, although Kawata's analysis filled Akiko with utter glee.

Even before the official start at ten AM, the MgRonald received four early calls, making the atmosphere tense around the kitchen. Emi's first job as call handler was thus to apologize to them, since their computer system wouldn't accept any orders before that time.

The first time she said "We have a web order in" over the headset, everyone on staff whose hands were free gave a round of applause to celebrate. In a few moments, Kawata was off with his heat-insulated delivery bag, specially developed for MgRonald's new program. Putting on his elbow and knee protectors, keeping his scooter key (with plastic tag and anti-loss code) on his belt, he flew out the door for his first delivery.

Five minutes later, another online order showed up. Immediately after that:

"Thanks for calling MgRonald at Hatagaya station. This is Yusa speaking. How can I help you?"

The first phone order was in.

"If I could have your address and phone number, please… All right. So to confirm your order, I have a Double Full-Moon Burger Set with… Okay. At the current time, we're looking at…"

Typing in the information with practiced hands, Emi checked the order's delivery address and switched to in-house headset mode.

"Same direction, toward Sasahata District five. Less than five minutes apart."

"Can you take 'em both, Marko?" Kisaki broke in.

"Roger that," said Maou as he inserted the two complete orders into his own bag.

"Do you know the way?"

"Yeah, I think I know the roads over there. This is the phone number?"

He gave another look at the receipt Emi handed him, then checked the map of their delivery area hanging on the nearby wall.

"Here, huh? If it's district five, then order number eleven should be near the bottom of that steep hill. Number twenty-one… Okay, I got it. I'll let you know if something comes up."

"All right. See you later."

"………Yeah."

The sight of Emi giving him a perfectly normal smile as she waved him off was almost surreal. But he had a job to do, so Maou filed the thought away, put on his helmet, and set off. He could feel Akiko's dubious gaze out the corner of his eye; this, too, he ignored as he hopped aboard the brand-new Honta Gyro-Roof out front. Turning the key, he was rewarded with an engine roar that immediately conjured memories of his most recent time in Ente Isla.

"We are off! Onward, Red Dullahan I!!"

Having already prenamed the restaurant bikes Red Dullahan I, II, and III in his mind, Maou gave this new steed a heroic bit of encouragement as he set off into the mean streets of Sasazuka and Hatagaya.

"Not as many as anticipated, huh?"

"No. Considering the number of early birds, I was hoping for a few more, but… Ah, well."

Emi and Kisaki were manning the front counter, devoting themselves to their usual duties. The lunch rush was over, but they were still hovering at a total of just ten delivery orders so far. They were prepared for the worst, the entire staff ready and willing to tackle whatever came their way, but the numbers were something of an anticlimax.

"Well," Kisaki said, "we wouldn't want the system blowing up on the first day anyway. Let's call today a break-in day. Plus, it's nice out. It's good to have easy weather on the first day, but we'll tend to get more orders when it's bad outside. If we get rain during a short-staffed period, that's when we'll really prove our worth."

It was a tad ironic, the way they were too prepared to kick this thing off, but there wasn't much to be done about it. Maou had just returned from dropping off order number ten, ahead of Kawata, who was still busy ferrying the ninth one over.

"Welcome back, Marko."

"Anything to note out there?" Emi asked.

"It was some kind of student gathering," commented Maou. "I couldn't tell who owned the place, so I can't say too much about the customers. It's a pretty narrow road leading up to the apartment building, but there was a ton of traffic on it, so maybe make a note of that. Instead of parking right at the building, it'd be safer to park a bit early and walk the rest of the way."

"All right. I'll type that in."

The computer system let users type in notes about customers and deliveries to help teams keep track of and share information. Emi had almost finished typing "Heavy traffic in area, be careful when parking" when the phone rang. The three of them exchanged glances before Emi turned back to her computer.

"Thanks for calling MgRonald at Hatagaya station. This is Yusa speaking. How can I help you?"

"Hey, Kawatchi isn't back yet?"

"He got sent to the far end of our delivery radius," Kisaki said as she watched Emi. "That'll be a lot of narrow roads and one-way streets to navigate…"

Then she stopped…

"…!"

…because Emi herself had frozen solid at her station, letting out a light gasp. She made a habit of smiling when dealing with customers over the phone, but now her face was taut with concern.

"…Maybe a prank?" Maou asked Kisaki.

"I dunno…"

They hadn't received any prank calls or deliveries to nonexistent locations yet. *This might be the first one*, Maou thought.

"…All right. So that'll be two Big Mag meals…"

Maou raised an eyebrow as Emi fell back into the usual phone procedure. That was weird. With all her call-center experience, a regular old prank call shouldn't faze her as much as this one obviously did. He had no idea why she reacted like that, out of the blue. But she completed the order anyway, printing out a receipt for a fairly hefty order totaling nearly five thousand yen.

"You okay, Saemi? Something startle you?"

Kisaki, for her part, was more concerned than chiding about Emi's transformation. But she just shook her head. "No, it's nothing. This one's headed for Sasazuka, Maou."

"Oh, okay."

If it was nothing, that didn't explain the stiffness in her voice. Did the guy on the other end of the line say something creepy to her?

Emi took a deep breath. "It's really nothing," she whispered, so only Maou could hear. "I'm fine."

"Emi..."

"Ms. Kisaki's recognized me as part of the team. I gotta at least handle something like this with a smile. I'm sorry, I guess I need some more experience."

"Oh, no, it's fine, but... Hmm?"

Emi handed Maou the receipt. He reflexively checked the address and phone number on it. It almost made his eyes pop out. *Now* he knew what was up.

"Uh, this..."

Emi shook her head at the slightly agitated Maou. "It's just our job."

"All set, Marko," came Kisaki's voice. "Head on out."

"Oh, uh, sure thing."

"Be careful."

Maou wasn't too sure what, exactly, Emi wanted him to be careful about. But he still scowled at himself as he adjusted his helmet strap before starting up Red Dullahan I. Order number eleven for the day, it turned out, was headed for Villa Rosa Sasazuka, Room 101, and not even Maou could drum up a polite smile for *that* destination.

"Who the hell even called that in?"

He couldn't guess from Emi's gasp, but unless this was some trick, it had to be Nord Justina, Room 101's only official resident. But that shouldn't elicit such a negative reaction from her.

"It's gotta be Laila, huh? She is *such* a goddamn prick."

No, this wasn't Laila beating a path down to his front door, or to their workplace. Instead, it'd be her forcing them to *her* doorstep. Maou and Emi were employees of the MgRonald Corporation, and if a customer called in an order, they had to deliver it. Villa Rosa Sasazuka was firmly within delivery range. No way to avoid it.

"Oops. This is a one-way street?"

The path he navigated countless times on foot or bicycle now looked very different to him on a scooter. The route to his "delivery destination" was just a bit more circuitous than what he'd usually take. When he arrived, it almost felt like someone else's building.

"My liege? Why are you here?" Ashiya was just coming down the stairs when he marveled at the sight of Maou on his scooter. "Did you forget something?"

"This is for work, man," he said as he removed his helmet and pointed at the container on his back. "I'm delivering to '*Mr. Sato*' in Room 101."

"You…?"

Ashiya immediately picked up on the intention behind the order.

"That accursed angel! The sheer arrogance of summoning the Devil King himself with a single telephone call!"

"Well, when you put it that way… But if I've got this uniform on, I've got a job to do—and I can't bad-mouth my customers behind their backs. So let it slide, okay?"

"But perhaps, if I could join you…?"

"I don't need backup to deliver some burgers, man. I've already done this a bunch of times today. I'll hand the food over, they'll give me the money, and I'll leave. That's all. Just do whatever you were planning to do. I left the MgRonald almost ten minutes ago; I gotta get this food to 'em hot."

"Your Demonic Highness…ngh… I feel it is a mistake, letting angels and humans comingle so closely with us… But please, do be careful! I cannot say what nefarious scheme they may hatch upon you!"

"Dude, for the twentieth time, it's just burgers! Go worry somewhere else. I'll be fine. Ah-*hem*!"

Clearing his throat as he left the agitated Ashiya, Maou marched over to Room 101 and pressed the doorbell button, demonstrating not a hint of hesitation. "Hello!" he shouted out, all business. "MgRonald delivery with your order!"

"Ah, thank you."

What he didn't expect was Nord Justina answering the door. He was sure it'd be Laila, or Gabriel, at least. It was almost a disappointment.

"Right, thank you for waiting. Let me give you your drinks first... and here is your Big Mag and medium fry sets. Be careful; it's hot."

"...I thought you would refuse the order. Or send someone else, at least."

"I would never refuse a valid order, sir."

Exchanging a few pleasantries with customers at the delivery site was another part of the job. When Maou first saw Nord, his Japanese language ability was at about on par with Acieth's, but now he was showing quite a bit more fluency. Perhaps being reunited with Emi gave him more contact with the language; maybe Laila sprinkled some pixie dust or whatever to bring him up to native level. Maou pondered this as he peered over Nord's shoulder, hoping to see if anyone else was inside—but Room 101 was too dimly lit to discern very much.

"...All right. Does everything in the order look correct?"

"Yes, thank you."

"You're welcome. Your total today comes to 4,530 yen."

The five-thousand-yen note Nord handed him seemed normal enough. Maou took some change from his waist pouch, counted it out, and gave it to him with his receipt.

"Thank you very much for your order! We look forward to serving you again."

"Mm-hmm."

Everything was just like all the other orders so far. He began to zip his insulated bag back up.

"Oh, one more thing... Maou?"

"...........Yes?" he replied, turning his head back around. It was still the same old Nord there, face serene.

"I wanted to ask you something about this flier."

"...What's that?"

Maou noticed Ashiya looking from afar, almost dying from the suspense of what might happen to his master. He ignored him, devoting his attention to his customer.

"It says here that you're hiring, but are you still looking for people?"

"…?"

Maou's eyebrows drilled downward. *What? He can't possibly want to apply for a part-time job at MgRonald?*

"I've been delivering newspapers for a long time. I think I have a good knowledge of the city streets, and I'll be earning my own scooter license soon. What do you think?"

That *was* the whole reason they found each other in the first place, wasn't it? On that bus headed for the license test center.

"I think," Maou said, choosing his words carefully, "we are still looking for employees, but it might be better to ask directly at the location. I'm sure Ms. Kisaki, the manager, would be glad to talk to you."

"I see. All right. Sorry to delay you."

"Not at all. Thank you very much."

With a light nod, Nord ended the conversation and shut the door.

Even in the middle of his work, Maou had set all five of his senses (plus magic) to work. They told him that Laila wasn't around. Neither was Gabriel, nor Shiba or Amane.

"M-my liege?" Ashiya asked, immediately sprinting over.

"Talk about having the rug pulled out from under you. Nothing happened."

"It did not? But he appeared keen on applying for a job, there in the end."

"If he decides to, then yeah, that's gonna suck…but that's up to Ms. Kisaki to decide, and it's not really anything I can comment on. I mean, maybe he was targeting me during work so I wouldn't lie to him, but what's the point of summoning me here to ask such a basic question?"

If Nord applied for work at the Hatagaya station MgRonald, Maou's first concern would be how he'd interact with Emi. But regardless of how badly Laila was screwing things up, Emi undoubtedly loved Nord as a father. It might even be a good way to get them talking to each other again.

Either way, though, it had nothing to do with Maou, and if Nord didn't have his license yet, he might not even score the job in the first place.

"...Ah, well. Back to work."

"My liege, perhaps I could corner him and attempt to extract the truth from—"

"No. If the tenants here start fighting each other, you *know* our landlord's gonna swoop right in."

"Dehh...!"

Ashiya gnashed his teeth, mortified. Maou, despite his rebuke, didn't like it, either. It felt weird, like a sesame seed stuck between his teeth. "I feel," he reflected, "like a puzzle piece getting jammed into a puzzle I don't fit."

"But my liege, would it not be best to simply continue with our current approach, to ignore whatever tricks they throw upon us? There is no need for us to so much as lift a finger to help them."

"Yeah, I guess you're right." Maou nodded at him before returning to Red Dullahan I and putting his helmet back on. "Hey, do *you* wanna make an order? I could use my phone to get it sent out here."

"I apologize, Your Demonic Highness, but I have already prepared our meals up to tomorrow's lunch."

"Okay. Just don't let Emi sneak into our kitchen again, like that one night. I almost had a heart attack."

His eyes grew hazy as he recalled the events.

"I apologize, my liege. I never expected she would commit such a brazen act while we slept. Having Emilia lay her hands upon our store of rice is the greatest embarrassment of my life..."

"Brazen...? Well, yeah, they were shaped a little weird, but they tasted fine. They weren't laced with poison or anything."

"Indeed, my liege, and that makes it even more terrifying. Why would Emilia Justina go out of her way to prepare rice balls for the Devil King? I cannot imagine what her motivation could possibly be."

"Her brain probably fried or something."

He hadn't told anyone what had happened that night. He doubted Emi had.

"But hey, no trouble since then, right? And hell, maybe Nord just got a hankering for some fast food. You never know. But I better get going."

"Ah, yes, my liege. My apologies. Please drive safely."

With the respectfully bowing Ashiya behind him, Maou took his leave of Villa Rosa Sasazuka. He spent the trip back to MgRonald thinking about the past week. He was right—since the subway attack on Emi and Chiho, nothing particularly bad had happened to anyone. Emi's "brain crash" was a deadly serious accident in Maou's eyes, but fortunately, it didn't seem like Alas Ramus or Acieth got wind of those events at all. Emeralda was still with Emi in Eifuku-cho, and Amane and Shiba didn't seem up to much of anything. The subway attack must've knocked the wind out of Laila's sails, too; the last time Maou saw her was when she paid a single visit to the apartment, two days after Emi's brain crash. Her hair was still purple, but Maou didn't care to find out why, or even where she was living.

"Nothing better than the same ol', same ol', huh?" he muttered amid the whine of the engine.

Back at the restaurant, Maou was greeted by the concerned Emi and Chiho, who had just arrived for her shift.

"Maou?" Chiho said as she ran up to him. "Are you okay? Emi told me you went to Room 101 for a delivery…"

"What did my father want from you?" Emi asked, her face ashen.

"Well, about that…"

He gave them a quick recap.

"So really, except for Nord asking me about a job, there was nothing unusual about it. I was all but expecting Laila and Gabriel to surround me and lock me up in there, but no. It was Nord who called you, wasn't it, Emi?"

"…Yeah."

"Because you looked really pained about it. Like, you made this *really* freaky face. That's why I was so concerned."

"Freaky? Freaky how?" Emi scowled, then thoughtfully tilted

her head. "It felt like the order was too much for just one person, so I thought Laila was bound to be behind him. That's why I was so tensed up..."

"Yeah, it *was* a lot."

Four thousand five hundred and thirty yen was far above the average bill for a trip to MgRonald. Even Sariel, back when he was eating three meals a day there in a vain effort to win Kisaki's heart, only rarely made an order that surpassed three thousand.

"Even if it was all meal sets, that'd still be, like, food for seven people, right?"

Delivery orders had an extra fee tacked on to them, so Nord's actual food order cost around 4,200 yen.

"You think he actually ate all that himself? He's not Acieth."

"Perhaps she was there to eat it with him," Chiho suggested.

"Maybe. I can't say if she's spending a ton of time in the same room that angel might show up in, though."

"She's living with Gabriel in Shiba's house, isn't she?"

"Yeah. My landlord's a saint for doing that. That's some *serious* labor, I tell you... Oh, speaking of which, Acieth made Rika Suzuki pay for this really huge dinner at MgRonald, but did she mention that to you?"

"What? No!" Emi's face tensed up again.

"She ordered forty burgers and four drinks, and Rika paid for it all."

The number made Chiho and Emi stare at him, astonished.

"I'm gonna have to apologize to her later... I really didn't want Rika to get any more involved in this stuff..."

"Well, too late now. Guess you could say those forty burgers are just collateral damage from the war on Ente Isla."

"Ha-ha-ha... But wow, Acieth really ate that? Forty burgers... I can't even imagine."

The topic of Acieth lightened the mood among all of them.

"But anyway, nothing set off any alarms with me. Let's get back to work."

"Okay!"

"True... Oop."

Just as she said it, Emi was greeted by a phone call in her headset. She jogged over to the delivery computer.

"Thanks for calling MgRonald at Hataga— Agh!"

Something on the line surprised Emi enough to stop her midsentence.

"..."

She looked at Maou and Chiho, face scrunched up like she'd just bit into the sourest thing in the universe, before reluctantly returning her attention to the call.

"Right, right... No, thank *you* for all your support. All right..."

"Your 'support'?" Chiho looked up at Maou, unsure who this could be.

"Certainly, yes...but if I may be honest, it's such a short distance away that I think you could save some money by coming here to pick it up—oh, you don't mind? All right... Um, *what*? Er, I apologize, we do not currently accept requests for particular delivery staff, so if you could just give me one moment to check on that? Thank you."

She grimaced for all the world to see as she put the call on hold and set the handset to in-store mode.

"Ms. Kisaki, we have a call from Mr. Sarue from Sentucky across the street."

""Uhh?"" Maou and Chiho groaned in tandem at the mention of the name. Speak of the devil, indeed. Or the angel.

"*...Sarue? What's he want?*"

Kisaki, upstairs covering the café while Maou was gone, was not pleased.

"He, erm, wanted to make a delivery order."

"*Is he insane?*"

Everybody on the crew, from Maou and Chiho on down, was in firm agreement. But the rival fast-food franchise was a whopping ten seconds' walk across the street. It was, technically, within delivery range.

"*So what? If he's willing to pay the delivery fee for taking it across the street, then fine, but if you're bringing this up with me, Saemi, does that mean he wants me to deliver it?*"

"...Yes."

"....................*Ugggggghhhhhh.*"

The entire staff swallowed nervously at the exaggerated sigh.

"*All riiiiiight. I'll just think of it as a business visit to advertise our new program. If they're in the same shopping arcade that we are, we gotta treat 'em like customers... It'd be ridiculous usually, but...*"

It certainly would be.

"*Tell Sarue...er, tell the customer that I'll be there. Is Marko back?*"

"Um, yes!" he called up the stairs at the sudden mention.

"*Okay. You take the café with Chi for me.*"

""""Understood!"""" the three employees chimed.

"Thank you for waiting. Ms. Kisaki will be handling the delivery, so I'm ready to take your order at.................. Um, I apologize, sir, but if you could keep your order to a size Ms. Kisaki can carry by herself..."

Sariel was probably wallowing in ecstasy. Emi tapped away at the keyboard, nodding at the voice on the line, as the receipt grew longer and longer. The final invoice made Kisaki visibly cringe when she went downstairs.

"My God, is he trying to break my back with all these burgers?"

The order almost made it up to ten thousand yen, forcing the delivery estimate to be twenty minutes despite the minuscule distance involved.

"...Well, there are people out there who can actually eat that much. Nothing weird about it."

"I hope Sariel doesn't start gaining weight again. Can one person really tackle this?"

"He can't be forcing the Sentucky employees to eat them. That'd be one crazy power trip."

Realizing that Sariel was, well, his usual self was, in some small way, reassuring to Maou. Especially at a time like this.

It was fair to say that the first day of MgRonald's delivery service was smooth sailing. They handled a total of thirty deliveries, twelve of which (including Nord's and Sariel's) were phoned in, proving Kisaki's theory correct. Scooter round trips tended to average around twenty minutes, and they'd likely be building their future operations on these first-day stats. For now, the next major obstacles to tackle would be (a) days with inclement weather, and (b) days without Maou, Kawata, or Emi, the main trio behind Day One's stellar performance.

"Ahhhh, it sure tired me out," Maou commented to Emi, stretching in the middle of the quiet shopping street afterward. "Having all that stuff I'm not used to yet happen at once, y'know?"

"True. I hadn't done call-center stuff in a while, so I got so nervous, my shoulders are sore."

"It's been a while since we had so much staff on hand, too. Man, we're seriously gonna miss Kota, though."

"Kota? You mean Nakayama? Is he quitting?"

Chiho, still a high schooler, could only work until ten PM. On this first day though, Kisaki, Maou, Kawata, Akiko, and Emi were all on shift until eleven thirty, when the MgRonald stopped taking orders. They were joined by Kotaro Nakayama, who would be leaving shortly to seek a full-time job.

"Yeah, he's job hunting postcollege. A guy with prospects like him, you can't make him work part-time forever. He's been here the whole time I have, though, so it's been nice to have someone to rely on when he's in my shift. I think the whole team's gonna miss him."

"Is Kawata going, too? He's the same year as Kota, I think."

"Not while he's still studying. He's got a family restaurant he'll be taking over when he graduates. I think he could do a lot of other things, though... Well, take care."

Maou took the Dullahan II out from the bike rack and prepared to set off.

"...What?"

He was stopped by Emi tugging at her bag.

"I need to pick up Alas Ramus at Bell's room. Let's walk back together."

"………Huh? Your brain about to crash again?"

He gave her the biggest wince he could muster. It didn't work much.

"You know the kid'll like seeing us together."

What had gotten *into* her since that night? This wasn't something as simple as her softening up a bit. Ever since that spine-tingling night, Emi had begun to show all kinds of new, and unfamiliar, emotions to Maou. She had become a completely changed woman over the past few days, with almost none of the high-pressure attitude that defined her in the past. She was all smiles when she dropped Alas Ramus off with Suzuno in the morning, a display that shocked the entire Devil King's Army.

Was Chiho picking up on this change? Keeping Emi and Maou on good terms with each other was one of her greatest priorities in life. Seeing Emi begin to meet him halfway must have been a dream come true for her. But to Maou, who couldn't understand what drove or motivated Emi to step up like this, the idea of giving her any concessions was unthinkable—just as it was when Suzuno became oddly friendly with her in Ente Isla.

"She's gotta be sleeping by now… Hmm?"

Wearily taking out his phone, he noticed a couple of new texts.

"Chi, and… Who's this?"

It was an unfamiliar number. And all it said was: "Come home at once."

"Yo, Emi, this text got sent to you, too."

"I know," she grimly replied. "I just saw it. Ring any bells?"

"Nope. No, but…"

He had the sneaking feeling he had seen this mystery contact before. It was a long time ago by now, but he remembered how Chiho sent a text right after *that* one, too.

"Well, not like there are too many people who'd send you and me a text like this."

"No."

"…You all right?" he asked, noticing the hangdog look on Emi's face as she put her phone back in her bag. The sender of that text was almost certainly going to be waiting at the apartment, and he was worried Emi wouldn't be ready for it.

"I'm fine," she insisted. "I'm not gonna give you that ugly act again." Maou was unsure about this, but she still gave him a firm nod. "If we have to deal with any more stupid crap, though, I'm not gonna have too much mercy this time."

"Well, don't overdo it."

"Oh, thanks for the kind words. I thought you didn't have time for weaklings."

"Quit dredging up stuff from the past. I'm just saying, if you start getting weepy again, it's gonna suck for me." He gave a half smile at this show of force from Emi. "I dunno who it is, but no need to hurry back. You know what? I'll take your invite. Let's go home together."

"All right. Wanna buy some *oden* snacks at the convenience store on the way?"

It strayed a fair distance from the Hero and the Devil King's usual conversations—or Maou and Emi's, for that matter—but it continued as they started walking to Villa Rosa Sasazuka. Emi looked up into the sky, taking in the creaking noise from the Dullahan II's chain.

"What did Chiho text you about, though? She didn't send one to me."

"The same thing, pretty much."

"Huh?"

Maou didn't return Emi's quizzical stare, keeping his eyes locked forward.

"They're waiting at the apartment."

"Damn, the gang's all here, huh?"

Upon reaching the building, Maou and Emi found Chiho, Ashiya, Suzuno, and Emerada waiting in the front yard, along with Gabriel, Nord, Shiba, Amane, and Alas Ramus in Acieth's arms. Urushihara, still a bit spooked about Shiba, was looking on from the safety of the stairwell, but otherwise, nearly everybody with a connection to Villa Rosa Sasazuka was on the lawn.

"You okay being out this late, Chi?"

"I was the one who called Ms. Sasaki over," Shiba declared.

"...You did?"

Why would she do that?

"It's fine with her folks, mm-kay? I followed all of Mikitty's instructions to make sure nobody got mad about it."

"If something happens to her parents later, I'm gonna kill you, Gabriel."

The ever-flippant angel was being brutally stared down by Acieth, standing next to Amane.

"Did you, um, send that text, ma'am?"

"Mm-hmm! I sent the same one to Ms. Yusa as well."

"I don't remember giving you my number. Plus..." Maou squinted his eyes at Shiba. "You sent me one before now, too, didn't you?"

"Mm-hmm," she breezily confessed.

Long ago, before Chiho knew about Maou's past and before Urushihara had even made it to Sasazuka, he had received what seemed to be an anonymous text warning him of imminent danger. Just like this one, in a way.

"I understand that Chiho Sasaki can harness the Idea Link through her cell phone, but, ah, you could say I did roughly the same thing. At the time, I didn't have the spare time to handle the Sephirah I contacted, and I had to oversee all of Japan by myself, so I'm afraid that was the best method I could think of."

"Because you already knew we were on Earth."

Maou sighed softly. So *that* was how long Shiba had been operating behind the scenes, pursuing Emi and him and everything that loomed behind them.

"So why are all of you here?"

"'Fraid things have changed a bit," Amane said. "Aunt Mikitty and I, you know, we can't provide you with unwavering support."

"What do you mean?"

"Go inside. You'll see." She pointed at Room 101. "We're gonna need to have you and Yusa there listen to her story."

"What if I say no?"

"Well, then it'll be up to me, Aunt Mikitty, and as many of our family members as we can assemble to kick you guys' asses offa Earth. If you're gonna keep bringing trouble to *this* planet, we'd really prefer if you chilled out over in *yours* instead."

She sounded serious.

"On the other hand, if you're willing to stay up a bit late tonight, step inside Room 101 and hear her out, we'll stay totally hands-off with ya. Think of this as, uh, negotiating your new rental contract."

"Wow, way to spring that on me." Maou shrugged, face taut. "You just want me to listen? That's it?"

"That's it. Right, Auntie?"

"Mm-hmm!" Shiba nodded at them. "And I think you'll find that she's doing her best to support your world, as well. I don't think she'll make the same mistakes again."

"She'd better not," Maou griped at no one in particular, "if she's carrying that much on her back. Otherwise, we're screwed." He patted Emi on the back. "Let's go."

"...Okay."

Emi looked just as stressed about this. But she was stable, far more than she was in Urushihara's hospital room.

Chiho looked on as they walked by. "Maou... Yusa..."

"My liege, do be careful..."

"Dude, whatever you do, don't make it so I have to get a job, okay?"

"Devil King!" Suzuno shouted. "Emilia! If you detect *anything* untoward in her attitude, do not so much as give her the time of day, do I make myself clear?"

"Daddy..."

Then Alas Ramus said something very strange indeed:

"Don't...hurt her, okay?"

What could she be afraid of? She knew already, or should have, that Emi took a firm, unbending attitude with Laila. But she seemed to be talking about something else now. There was no time to think about it. On the other side of that door, it would all make sense, hopefully.

Maou grabbed the knob on the Room 101 door he had stared down a few hours ago in his MgRonald uniform. He noticed light coming out from inside. Then:

"Wha...?!"

"What is...this...?"

They were greeted with a sight they never could have anticipated.

"I'm sorry to call you for this late at night. Would you mind coming inside?"

Maou and Emi were too dumbfounded to follow the command, instead standing at the front door in silence. They were expecting to see Laila on the other side of the door, of course; her hair was still tinted purple, but that was no urgent concern. What *was*, was the boy she had sleeping in a futon next to her.

It was a child they both were familiar with, one with a single shock of red coursing down his otherwise black hair. His skin was a dull, dark brown—not by birth, or following a vacation in the tropics, but almost like a bar of iron exposed to rainwater for too long. An unhealthy sort of rust seemed to cover his whole body. Only his left arm, naked and sticking out from the futon, was the color they remembered him being.

Maou said the name first.

"Erone...?!"

This was Erone, embodiment of the Sephirah known as Gevurah. He first appeared before them accompanying the Malebranche chieftain who visited Japan; Ashiya later learned he was working as a servant for Raguel and Camael. He was notably absent, however, in Efzahan and during Maou's battle against the angels, even after he had well and truly trounced them.

"Amane and Shiba found him for me, this afternoon."

Maou, hearing this, looked around Room 101 one more time. In one corner was a trash bag filled with the paper cartons and such from his lunchtime MgRonald delivery.

"Yes, I ordered that to feed him."

"He looks pretty weak. You think fast food was the best medicine for him?"

He couldn't help but sound a bit critical. Laila shrugged it off.

"Acieth and Alas Ramus seem to like it well enough. They're the ones who suggested it, and if it was the children of Sephirah endorsing it, I didn't think it could be that bad."

"Yeah, but even if he was healthy, nobody should eat *that* much at once…"

"Besides, 'weak' isn't how I would describe him. He has lost some of his stamina, yes, after that scuffle with Amane and the rest, but I think his biggest issue right now is just an upset stomach. He wolfed the entirety of that bag down as if it were nothing."

""Uh?""

This startled both Maou and Emi. They knew exactly how much Nord ordered, after all.

"Are all the Sephirah really that damn hungry?" Maou asked. "Alas Ramus isn't gonna wind up like that someday, is—?"

"Of—of course not!" Emi exclaimed, the mere idea horrifying her. "And that doesn't matter right now! What do you want from us? We have work tomorrow! Just spell out what you're after!"

Maou expected Emi's sharp tone to make Laila waver again, like she did before. Instead, she nodded resolutely.

"Before I do, I need to say some more about this child…Emilia."

Her voice trailed off a bit at the end. Emi picked up on it. "Don't call me by my name," she retorted, "like you're my friend or something."

Laila sighed a lonely sigh, then gave Erone's hair a light caress.

"This child was behind the dark shadow that attacked the subway Chiho Sasaki was riding."

""!""

Emi and Maou gasped in unison.

"Satan. This child ran away during all the chaos in Efzahan. He didn't want to be forced into a fight with Acieth Alla. He decided to serve the angels with his own free will, but the idea of engaging in combat with his fellow Sephirah was just too much to bear. So he ran. He ran all the way to Japan, where there were at least a few people who knew about him."

"Well, sorry to hear that. And he didn't get caught in my landlord's Sephirah fishing nets?"

"Ms. Shiba immediately detected him, yes. But Erone was already transforming by that time. It proved too difficult to track him. Emilia, that dark shade you saw is what happens when a Sephirah goes out of control—when they lose sight of the world they were put in place to protect. Gevurah governs all metallic elements, and having that manifest itself made his body so solid, not even your Better Half could cut through it. The metal was eating into his very conscious, but it was still attracted to the nearest Sephirah it could detect."

"…And what's this comic book superhero origin story have to do with *your* problem?"

"Don't you see?" a crestfallen Laila pleaded. "I'm worried that Alas Ramus and Acieth are going to wind up like Erone."

The statement seemed designed to heavily impact Maou and Emi, who knew more about Ente Isla's Sephirah than most. But Maou wasn't buying it.

"Me and Emi are supposed to be their 'latent forces' or whatever. Why would they turn out like this boy here?"

"A Sephirah who selects a latent force is stable, yes. But a latent force is not permanent. If that force dies, the child will be left all alone—and they may decide to abandon you as a latent force, too. If they do, there is a nonzero chance of becoming…unstable, like this. The Da'at which guides these children hasn't been born in their world yet."

More of that stupid jargon. Maou pressed on, ignoring it.

"So…what are you saying, lady? Like, 'listen to me, or else your kids'll look like this soon'?"

Laila shook her head. "I may have worded it differently before now, but it's the exact same thing I told you earlier, before you dismissed me. Satan, Emilia…I wanted to harness the love you have for the Yesod. I thought that love was a given."

She adjusted her position, kneeling on the tatami-mat floor so she was directly facing them.

"So I don't want you to listen to my story today. Instead, I want you to perform a job for me."

""A job?"" the Devil King and the Hero asked in unison.

Laila nodded, then showed them a small stack of letter paper she had prepared in advance.

"This is an outline of our business plan, our compensation structure, and a draft version of our contract."

Maou and Emi gave each other a look. There was Laila, kneeling and firmly staring at them—none of the wavering indirection from that hospital room.

"What I want you to do is this: I want you to come with me and bring Ente Isla back to the way it should be. In exchange, I will provide you with suitable compensation. And I promise I will do nothing to negatively affect your lives here."

"Wh-what are you talking about?"

"Of course, I don't need you to agree right this minute. No... In fact, don't. I want us to thoroughly talk this over until we find some conditions we can all agree to. And if we can't come to an agreement in the end, you can just pretend you never heard any of this. I won't mind."

They could both tell. The resolve present in every word of Laila's proposal was a far cry from anything before.

".........And what if we turn you down?" Emi asked, her voice quivering.

Laila shook her head again. "If you can't accept it, then don't worry about anything after that. This might sound like sour grapes to you, but I'm sure you have better things to do than keep tabs on a contract you never intended to sign up for."

"Yeah, good point."

Maou casually nodded—quite a different reaction from the fairly shocked Emi—and looked back toward the closed door.

"Did Gabriel put you up to this?"

"No," Laila said. "It was you, Satan."

"Huh?"

"What?"

"I don't remember anything that happened in that subway tunnel. I was already here when I woke up. My hair color was a surprise, but Emeralda told me that Satan was the one who healed me."

"…Yeah."

"I woke up in the middle of the night, and even then, my wounds didn't hurt at all. I was thirsty, so I got up for a drink of water…and I could hear your voice, Satan."

Maou rolled his eyes. Then he hung his head in shame.

"What'd you hear first…?"

"The part about steel plates."

He rubbed his forehead with his hand.

"Until that point, I never truly understood how foolish, how shallow I was. You aren't the same as when I knew you. You're a wonderful grown man. But perhaps I've lived for so long that I didn't see you as an equal before."

Her voice, and her lips, were quivering. But she never turned her eyes away.

"So if you'll listen to me, I'll try as much as I can to provide whatever conditions you want. I can't assist you in conquering the world, Satan, but anything else within the realm of common sense…"

"Common sense to whom?"

"You know what I mean," Laila told Emi, her tone friendly. "I can provide anything, up to and including my own life."

Emi gasped.

"Emilia, as a mother and as a human being, what I did to you was unforgivable. Even killing me might not be enough to make up for all the hardships you've dealt with in your life. But if you still want my life, I will accept that."

"—?!"

The sight of her mother offering up her life threw Emi for a severe loop. Maou patted her on the back again, snapping her out of it. She looked up to find Maou frowning at her.

"Don't take it so seriously, dumbass," he spat out. "What a bunch of nonsense. Quit making this into a huge deal over crap that's never gonna happen anyway."

"But I'm serious. I just wanted to say, that's how resolved I am about this. And if you ever really do want my life, I'll follow through with that promise at all costs."

It was a crazy thing to say, but turn it around, and it meant she was willing to concede pretty much anything else "within the realm of common sense," no matter how extreme.

"Why are you going so far?"

"Because I want to protect the future of everyone who lives in that beautiful world, Ente Isla. That's half of it. The other half is, I want to exact judgment upon the sinners."

It was a concise enough answer. And even if Maou didn't know who she meant by "sinners," he had only one reply to it:

"All right."

"Hmm?"

"I'll sit down at the bargaining table for you, at least."

"You will?! Satan!"

"Devil King! What are you trying to do?!"

Emi tried to grab Maou by the collar as Laila beamed, rising to her feet.

"But before I do! Before I do, there's something I wanna say... Let *go* of me, Emi."

"I *said*, what are you trying to do?!"

"I'll tell you, so let me go! You're gonna stretch out the collar."

Emi's lips made an inverse V shape as she complied. The disappointment in her eyes was clear as day to Maou.

"...Is this just, like, you're fine with anything as long as you get paid?" she said. "I gave you such a...window into my feelings, too..."

"Compensation is important. And she said she's ready to bargain with us on the conditions, yeah?"

"Well, yes..."

Laila blinked helplessly. She had no idea what Maou would say, and Emi's sudden hostility was a source of serious concern.

"And I don't know where you got that idea from, Emi, but I didn't say yes because I'm on *your* side or anything. I just don't like how these guys have handled everything so far, so I wanted to bitch at 'em about it."

"...!" Emi gasped again, no longer able to fully hide the shock on her face. Laila, looking a bit panicked herself for the first time, attempted to step in.

"S-Satan... Um, I know you and Emilia don't get along very well, but I was hoping I could get help from both of you, so...if you could..."

"If you know that, then why are you misunderstanding this, Laila? Like, right at the end, too. Her and I are enemies."

"You don't have to say it again!" Emi interjected. Maou responded by sticking his fingers in his ears, the universal "la-la, I can't hear you" signal.

"All right? So just because you've landed me, if you think Emi's just coming along as a bonus, you're dead wrong."

""...Huh?""

Both mother and daughter simultaneously voiced their shock. Maou paid them no mind.

"Lemme state a few conditions I want in place before I sit down to negotiate. It's all a hell of a lot more realistic than taking your life, so I'm not gonna take no for an answer."

He pointed a finger straight up.

"We'll conduct our negotiations in Room 201 of Villa Rosa Sasazuka, and I'll always have one other person accompanying me. This person will be one of the following four people: Ashiya, Urushihara, Chi, or Acieth inside me. Nobody else. Finally, no discussion is allowed anywhere except in that room. You have to accept all three of these conditions, or else I'm not gonna listen."

"Th-that's it? In that case, no problem."

It was anticlimactic for Laila, who was expecting the worst. But Maou left no stone unturned.

"Did you hear that, Emi?"

"Huh?"

"Laila's just agreed that, if she talks to me, she's gonna do it in Room 201 with me and either Ashiya, Urushihara, Chi, or Acieth."

"Y-yes…"

"Wh-what? It didn't sound unreasonable to me."

"And you can't tell me *anything* about your story outside of those conditions. If you do, it's all off the table. Got all that?"

"Of—of course. That's nothing."

Seeing Laila nod to her side, Emi turned to see an evil grin erupt upon Maou's face. Then he said something truly unimaginable.

"Y'know what, Emi? I think I'll take you up on that invite again."

""…Huh?"" Emi and her mother said.

"Let's go home together every day from now on."

For several moments, the only sound in Room 101 was Erone's slightly strained breathing as he slept.

"""""Huuuuuuuuuuuuhhhhhhhhhhhhhhhhhhhhhh?!"""""

Four screams sounded off at once, Emi's included.

"M-my liege! What has happened?!"

"D-Devil King?! What's going on?! Are you mad?! Have you caught a fever?!"

"Ma-Ma-Ma-Ma-Maou going, going home with Yu-Yu-Yusaaaa…"

Ashiya, Suzuno, and Chiho leaped for the door, all but ready to break it down.

"Guys, we got a kid recuperating in here… Plus, it's Nord's room…"

"That does not matter, Your Demonic Highness! My liege's mental health is a far more important issue than Nord Justina's front door!"

"Ashiya, our landlord's literally right there…"

"Yes," said Suzuno, "I may have told you to lend a sympathetic hand to Emilia, but what has *happened* to you both in the past few days?! You all but kicked Rika and myself out of the restaurant not long ago. What is the meaning behind this vast change of heart?!"

"You're digging your own grave, Suzuno. And that topic of conversation pains me, too, so could you drop it?"

"I-I-I-I'm glad you and Yusa are getting along and—and—and stuff," Chiho managed, "but, um, um, I wasn't expecting you to get *this* close. Like, maybe I was arrogant, but it's just so *ridiculous*, but—but Yusa's a good friend of mine, too, so if that's what you want, Maou, I..."

"Chi, Chi, calm down. Your face is going crazy."

"......What.........did you say...?"

Among her three panicked acquaintances, Emi was the most lost at sea, her face bright red itself.

It was, perhaps, for the better that Urushihara hadn't inserted himself into this scene of mass panic, but he was likely the only one who understood Maou's intention behind this. Or perhaps not, on second thought. Regardless, Maou patted Chiho's shoulder, lest she break something with all the facial contortions she was making, and whispered into her ear:

"The shift schedule."

"I...I... Huh?"

"Remember the shift schedule."

"The shift...schedule...?"

"The shifts... Ah?!"

Before Chiho could retrieve the Hatagaya station MgRonald schedule from her memory, Ashiya somehow came to the conclusion first.

"You and Emilia are always working the same shifts, my liege?"

"Huh?! ...Ah!"

Before they could ask why Ashiya was so intimately familiar with not only Maou's schedule but that of every other employee at MgRonald, Chiho finally caught up with the gist.

"We come in at different times, but—yeah, we usually both get off at the same time, and we get the same breaks 'n' stuff. The older ladies fill in a lot of the gaps on the weekends, so... For this month, at least, me and Emi are almost always there together, until everyone gets in the groove with the delivery service."

Leaving the still-dazed Chiho behind for a moment, he turned to Laila.

"And like I said, if I hear *anything* about this outside of the conditions I gave you, I'm out. No help from me at all. You agreed to that, so don't try to weasel your way out of it."

Laila replayed the conversation in her mind.

"Ah, wait..."

The full brunt of the truth hit her.

"W-wait, wait a second! In that case, where am I supposed to talk to you?!"

"Hey, I got a few days off, too. I'll tell you when those are, so come on up when it's convenient for you. Ashiya and Chi have their own errands to run, but I guarantee that Urushihara's always gonna be at home, and Acieth's probably bored all day with my landlord, too. If you come here when I have off, you'll get my ear then, I all but guarantee it."

"N-no, no, it's not about that, or you; it's..." Laila's face reddened. Her breezy confidence was waning. "If—if I try to live up to those conditions..."

"Let me remind you, I can't sit around at work and listen to your long-winded nonsense. And Emi wasn't on my list of approved people to sit in with me. Neither is Suzuno or Alas Ramus."

"Wait, wait, wait, but that means...you know..."

"Devil King, you didn't...?"

Maou sized up the agitated Laila and Emi. He wasn't willing to listen alongside Emi—but for the foreseeable future, he'd be spending a fairly hefty chunk of every day with Emi. The chances of all Maou's conditions being met were slim to none—and as long as he and Emi were together, Laila couldn't make contact with Emi. And if she couldn't, how was Laila ever going to negotiate with her? She couldn't. Not without going over to Urban Heights Eifukucho herself.

"Wait... Wait! Devil King, I... This is all so sudden..."

"What, Emi? Are you saying you can't even have an argument with your own mother without me chaperoning? Some Hero you are."

"It-it-it's not that! What makes you think I can't talk to Laila if *you're* not around?! You—you know that's just stupid!"

"So it's fine, then."

"It's not fine, it's…! …Huh?"

"You can talk or fight or whatever all you want to when I'm not there. You're family, right?"

Emi stared, slack jawed, at Maou's face. She had just been blocked from bringing Maou into her negotiations. And not only was it blocked—the whole fact she had subconsciously included that possibility in her own choices jolted her.

"…All right. I'll do that."

"Emilia?!"

Maou gave her a taunting grin. "*Can* you?"

Cheeks now the color of cherries, Emi pointed a finger straight at Maou. "I am the Hero!" she declared. "I don't need any help from *you*, and I can negotiate this job all by myself! So don't treat me like some huge wimp!"

She had not loosened on her opinion of Laila, but falling straight into Maou's trap had riled her so much that she just had to say her piece. Nothing about it was rational thought. It was a reflexive reaction—but, looking at the outburst, Maou gave a satisfied nod.

"There's the Emi I know. What a relief."

Then, leaving the confused group behind, he stepped out of Room 101. The first person he addressed outside was Shiba.

"Hey, you sure that kid's gonna be okay in that room?"

"Laila said she would take responsibility for him. I'll do my best to check on him as well."

"Thanks." Then he turned to Emeralda. "I'm no longer involved with what went on over there, so just do whatever you want, all right?"

"Heh-heh-heh! Cerrrtainly." She bowed, beaming all the way. "I'll do whatever I can to help supporrrt Emilia."

"I just said, lady, whatever you want." Next was Acieth, holding Alas Ramus. "You come over to visit 'im sometimes, too. I know you got a lot of free time on your hands. Emi's keeping Alas Ramus here in this apartment, too."

Acieth nodded, giving him a stern look.

"Daddy…"

"Hey, it's all right. Once Erone wakes up, you make him apologize, all right?"

"Okeh!"

Finally, Maou called up to Urushihara, still hanging around the stairwell.

"Hey! What was for dinner tonight?"

"I 'unno. Ask Ashiya."

"You can't even remember *that*? Is that pork miso soup I'm smelling?"

"Dude, why'd you ask me if you knew all along? You act like I've got all the time in the world for you…"

"You mean you don't?"

Maou gave Urushihara a bop on the forehead for that one.

"Ugh, this month is gonna suuuuck, isn't it?"

"Guess so," Maou observed as Urushihara followed him upstairs.

"But hey, do you think that's gonna keep Laila 'n' Emilia in their place, though? You think this is just gonna make all those problems go away?"

"What do you mean?" Maou asked, whirling around to give him a tired look. Urushihara, hands clasped behind his head, just sighed.

"If I wind up comin' out of this looking like a prick, dude, it's *your* fault."

"Huhh?"

Amane yawned as she watched them disappear down the walkway. "Well," she offered, "Aunt Mikitty didn't say anything, so I guess she's gonna renew their lease."

"Oooh, he sure did it," Gabriel half growled, looking honestly peeved for a change. "He sure did it now, huh? Sure wasn't expecting that approach, hoo boy…"

Nord just looked on, perplexed, as he heard the door to Room 201 close.

"A mysterious man, indeed…"

EPILOGUE

In the end, Maou and Emi still knew nothing.

What had Laila been scheming for, all this time? After all the strange, inscrutable things Gabriel had gotten up to, why was he on Laila's side now? What role did the Sephirah children have in saving Ente Isla? How was the Tree of Sephirot holding up, locked away now in heaven?

But now that Maou and Laila had at least agreed to talk things over, one thing had palpably changed.

"I can't breathe!!"

"Silence, Urushihara. We are trying to eat here," Ashiya replied.

"It's too hot!!"

"Surely you jest, Lucifer. It is November. Almost time for me to change into my winter kimono sets," Bell added.

"Dude, Ashiya, Bell, you *know* what I'm trying to say! Quit ignoring me!"

""What could you possibly mean?"" the two asked simultaneously.

"Don't give me that crap!! Why the hell are there that many dudes in here?!!" Urushihara yelled, having finally lost his patience. "Acieth! Emeralda Etuva! Laila! Gabriel! Nord Justina! Get out of here, guys! Why do you all gotta eat dinner in our home, too?! This joint's tiny! You know that!!"

"Urushihara! You almost kicked over the table! This miso soup's gonna spill all over the place!"

"Chiho Sasaki! Don't you have any thoughts about this at all?!"

"Of course I do!!"

"Whoa!"

He reared back at the unexpectedly caustic reaction.

"But…but what do you want me to do about it?! I-I'm just so jealous! I wish I could substitute in for her! Never in my dreams did I think Yusa would…Yusa would wind up…like *this*…!!"

"Ch-Chiho, um, I'm sorry, but it's really nothing like that."

"Like *this*" seemed a rather rude way of putting it in Emi's mind. After all that yelling at Laila and Maou, she was now seated next to the devil himself, bowl in hand, not quite sure how she wound up here.

"I know!" Chiho replied, returning to her seat with a sort of half laugh, half sob. "I've always wanted you and Maou to be happy together! That's totally the truth!!"

She wolfed down some rice in a very impolite, non-Chiho-like manner that resulted in a few grains sticking to her cheeks, then glared menacingly at the woman next to her.

"Laila! If there's anybody I should resent, it's you, Laila!"

"Um, I don't know why, but sorry…"

The archangel controlling the fates of both Ente Isla and demon-realm history behind the scenes bore the brunt of the teenager's abject rage admirably well as she reached out for some pickled vegetables.

"Now, now, c'mon, guys, it's fun to eat in a big group like this, mm-kay? Quit worrying about your little squabbles 'n' stuff. And I've even brought along a little treat to add to the meal. Ta-da! Mikitty's handmade meatballs in sweet vinegar paste!"

Unlike the somber Laila who came empty-handed, the ever-gregarious Gabriel had taken a large plastic container out from a tote bag. It was filled, as promised, to the brim with large meatballs, filling the table with the soft scent of bean paste and paprika. He was by far the largest man in the group, and sitting cross-legged at the low table made him the target of repeated, merciless kicking from Urushihara.

"Dude, you're so huge, you're in my way! And this table's already too full of miso soup and rice bowls for your crap! And

I don't need handmade anything from that landlord! She already makes my hair bleach out; does she wanna do that with my soul next?!"

"Ooh, that's pretty rude there. Mikitty brought these out for everybody to share, too. She said it's high-grade Japanese Black beef from Kagoshima!"

"Apologize to Gabriel, Urushihara."

The mention of the fancy Wagyu breed made Ashiya immediately snatch up the container, put some meatballs on a plate, and toss them headlong into the microwave.

"Whoa! Maou! Ashiya's sold his soul as a Great Demon General for some stupid meatballs! We oughtta court-martial him!!"

"Ooh, no worries, Lucifer!" Acieth interjected. "If there are the extra, me and Eme take them!"

Urushihara cupped his head in his hands at the extremely unhelpful offer. "I'm not worried about that! And you guys eat too much, you know!"

"Maou! Please, would you exercise your rights as master of this domain and *do* something with these impudent fools?! And you as well, Emilia! This place is a battlefield every evening because *you* never show any resolve around here!"

".......Got me there," Maou muttered as he prodded his food.

Emi, shoehorned next to him, winced as she tried to put a response together. ".......I'm sorry, it's just..."

"It's fine, Emilia," came the calm, reassuring voice of Nord. "Nobody is forcing you. You must choose yourself. I will respect your and Laila's choices as much as I can."

"Father..."

"How 'bout you start respecting the choices of the people who actually live here, dude?!"

Next to the still-screeching Urushihara, another figure approached, making its way through the mass of bodies around the table.

"Lushiferr, sit down when you eat! That's mean!"

"Daaahhhhhhh!" the fallen angel groaned, incapable of chewing out a toddler.

It had been nearly five days since Erone was ferried into Room 101, and in that time, Emi had returned to her apartment in Eifu-kucho exactly once. Beyond that, she had been staying—intruding, really—in Suzuno's room. Laila had reportedly joined her on that single trip back home, but as Emeralda put it, things were so awkward between them that they could barely keep up a decent conversation.

It was the first chance to discuss matters, and not only did they both completely flub it—they hadn't even found a chance to talk, or fight, or even squabble since. Before they knew it, it was Laila, con-stantly searching for that instant when Emi was away from Maou's side, versus everybody else serving as security guards just in case things physically came to blows between the two. This banquet was the indirect result.

Maou had made his conditions in the first place for two reasons. One, he thought it best to keep himself and Emi separate when deciding whether or not to speak with Laila. Two, he wanted to stop worrying about Emi acting all irresolute about her mother, facing another brain crash, and throwing everything around her into con-fusion. If Emi and Laila could just face each other and talk, like two grown women, even if it resulted in no broad agreement, it'd at least help banish some of the hard feelings and bring Emi back to her old self.

That's what he had hoped for. Instead, he got this. Emi didn't have it in her to be alone with Laila at all. This was fine in itself, but she was now hiding herself in Maou's conditions for Laila, almost never leaving his side when she wasn't working with him. It was starting to make Maou miss the slay–the–Devil King, I-swear-I'll-kill-you, constant-nuisance, watching-behind-the-apartment-fence Emi of once upon a time.

Having this ball of mixed emotions next to him every waking hour made it impossible to figure out how to interact with her. He thought about taking a hard-line approach, but wasn't sure how; he had never done so before. Thus, the Devil's Castle had been completely full the past few days; the eerily observant Kawata and Akiko had been giving them strange looks at MgRonald; and the combination of Chiho's blazing eyes, Suzuno's frigid stares, Ashiya's despair as he watched all their rice disappear, and Urushihara's whining weighed all too heavily on his heart.

"Emi, can you at least take some responsibility for what you said? Were you really this gutless all along? Havin' a brain crash, or what?"

"I—I am not! I'm—I'm gonna talk it over. I am! Sometime..."

Every time Maou brought up the topic, it was always, "I'll do it sometime, I'll do it sometime."

"B-besides, it's not like *you're* ready to talk to Laila, either! You're having me come home with you after work so the conditions you set out for her never happen, aren't you...?"

"No, I'm not gonna deny that—but *only* for the distance between MgRonald and this apartment! I just didn't think the almighty Hero would wanna hang with demons after work and on all her off days, is all! Go home already!!"

He chose his words carefully to nettle Emi as much as possible. The reaction was even more visceral than he anticipated.

"I...! Wha...? I-it-it's not like I'm choosing to be with you! It's—it's just... You know, right now, things aren't...convenient right now..."

The incredibly inarticulate excuse, the lexical equivalent of falling on your face halfway across the street, ruined the atmosphere.

""""Not convenient how?"""" exclaimed Ashiya, Urushihara, and Suzuno all at once.

"H-hey! Did you just say something?"

""""No,"""" they exclaimed again, looking coldly off in the distance.

"I wanted Maou and Yusa to get along," observed Chiho, "and I guess my wish is half-true now, but...but, I dunno, this still doesn't feel totally right... I don't want to sound resentful or anything, but I just can't see much to be happy about... It's weird, Laila."

It was more her cursing out Laila at length than anything. The archangel was more or less next to her, chopsticks in her mouth, and Chiho spoke only loud enough for her to hear.

"No rest for the wicked," the utterly exasperated Maou muttered.

"Nor for I, Your Demonic Highness."

"You're right, Maou! I can't relax for a single moment!"

"I warned you about this, dude! Do something about it!"

"Indeed, everything has its limit…"

Maou and Emi's acquaintances each laid out their grievances in order. But it was Emi who landed the killer blow:

"I'm really sorry…but please, let me stay like this for a while longer…"

The whisper from the heart, as she sidled closer to Maou around the crowded table, shot across the room like lightning.

"Yu-Yu-Yu-Yu-Yu-Yu-Yu-Yusa?! Ummm?! Does, does that mean…?!"

"Whoa! Emi! Bollllld! Phewwww!"

"Emiliaaa, that could have been phrased farrr better, I thiiink."

Chiho nearly fainted on the spot. Acieth attempted to whistle her praises like a pumped-up football fan, but failed. Emeralda's face stiffened. And Maou said:

"Please, *please* don't bring any more trouble in here. Please…"

Maou turned white as a sheet, almost dropping his bowl and chopsticks entirely.

"Mommy 'n' Daddy are friends!"

Only Alas Ramus saw this as welcome news. Sadly, even her adorableness wasn't enough to lighten the mood.

And in Room 101:

"Hope they don't all fall through the ceiling."

Amane, checking up on Erone, glared upward, practically ready to burst with all the many, many sounds of life above.

"So they're choosin' dinner tonight over peace in the faraway future, huh? I should probably get somethin' to eat myself. He said I could help myself to the fridge, and I ain't about to say no to that."

Rubbing her hands together, she opened the door and began cobbling together an evening meal from the food inside. Erone, behind her, was groaning in his sleep. Was it a nightmare? Or was he just reacting to the noise above? There was no way to know until he woke up.

THE AUTHOR, THE AFTERWORD, AND YOU!

I have given serious thought in the past to why driver's license photos—and any ID photo, really—always turn out the way they do.

I, Wagahara, was already wearing glasses by the time I was old enough to need a picture ID. It's meant nothing but torment. Not only do I have to worry about my expression; if my frames are the slightest bit off-balance, then I've just wasted my money. Such a drag.

In the many years from my first student ID, through all the pics I've had taken for driver's licenses and résumés and such, I have never had a single one I could even describe as "not bad." Every time, there's always something that makes me audibly groan.

Back when I was involved in stage drama, my mentor told me that nobody's a worse actor than someone who literally thinks "Okay, let's do a good job acting this out." Dramatic expression begins to affect the viewer only when it retains the complex movements of the mind we all see in everyday life. There's nothing charming about someone who's only thinking about how to make themselves look as cool as possible. Looking back at my ID photos, that's the whole problem right there. All I want to do is *look good*, and the results are never gonna be convincing enough for me.

There's no way you can shoot one of those with a natural expression anyway. The face you make in them is a formality, a kind of ceremonious version of yourself you show to people. I've never seen anyone in real life make the allegedly "natural" expressions you see in photo IDs. So I thought, hey, if it's gotta be formal, I ought to at least put some enthusiasm in making it look as formal as possible. As a result, I'm still not too happy with my most recent license renewal, but at least I'm no longer agonizing about my facial expression.

With the new license holder in this volume, though, I'm sure he put entirely too much enthusiasm into his photo. It's a very lively pic, no doubt, one that just barely meets all the required standards. Sure hope it gets drawn for me.

Volume 12 of *The Devil Is a Part-Timer!* is the tale of some people who have something inside them that makes them constantly think about what it means to stand up and do something for someone, even as they scramble to keep food on the table. I sometimes have my concerns over whether I'm really giving back everything I receive from all my readers, but as long as I'm able to, I'm sure I'll manage to keep writing this story. Until we meet in the next volume, I'll do my best to give back everything I got.

See you then!

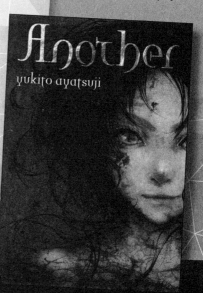